George Gordon Byron, James Thomas Hodgson

Memoir of the Rev. Francis Hodgson, B.D.

Scholar, Poet, and Divine. Vol. I

George Gordon Byron, James Thomas Hodgson

Memoir of the Rev. Francis Hodgson, B.D.
Scholar, Poet, and Divine. Vol. I

ISBN/EAN: 9783744691765

Printed in Europe, USA, Canada, Australia, Japan

Cover: Foto ©Raphael Reischuk / pixelio.de

More available books at **www.hansebooks.com**

REV. FRANCIS HODGSON, B.D.

MEMOIR

OF THE

REV. FRANCIS HODGSON, B.D.

SCHOLAR, POET, AND DIVINE

With numerous Letters from Lord Byron and others

BY HIS SON, THE

REV. JAMES T. HODGSON, M.A.

IN TWO VOLUMES

VOL. I.

London

MACMILLAN AND CO.

1878

PREFACE.

THIS MEMOIR has been compiled from a heterogeneous mass of letters and papers left, altogether without arrangement, by my father at his death in 1852.

A wish had for many years been entertained that some account should be placed on record of a life which, though devoid of stirring incident, was yet, from its connections and sympathies, full of varied interest. It was thought that enough of genius and culture were displayed by Francis Hodgson to entitle him to some biographical memoir, while his friendship with Lord Byron seemed to demand a more detailed description than any which could be derived from fragmentary allusions in the numerous notices of that most interesting life. It is hoped that a perusal of these pages may tend to remove several misconceptions, to clear away many clouds, which have hitherto prevented a just appreciation of the character of Byron.

At the outset of my undertaking I was met by two unusual deficiencies. Modern biography depends in the main upon one or other of two sources of information, personal recollections or original letters. Neither of these advantages could I command, and I have therefore been obliged to depart considerably from the method usually adopted. Acting on the principle that a man may more accurately be known by his friendships than in any other way, I have endeavoured to make the letters of friends, as far as possible, illustrative of the life and character of their correspondent; while, by indicating mutual opinions on matters of contemporary interest, I might contribute to the development of some aspect of the period social, political, or literary.

That such a novel mode of procedure is liable to much adverse criticism I am well aware : whether the end has in any measure justified the means must be left to the consideration of the reader.

CONTENTS

OF

THE FIRST VOLUME.

CHAPTER I.

CHAPTER II.

1794-1807.

CHAPTER III.

1807-1808.

CHAPTER IV.
1808.

CHAPTER V.
1808-1809.

CHAPTER VI.
1810.

CHAPTER VII.
1811.

CHAPTER VIII.
1811.

CHAPTER XIII.

1813–1814.

MEMOIR

OF THE

REV. FRANCIS HODGSON, B.D.

CHAPTER I.

FAMILY HISTORY—VAUGHANS—COKES—MOTHER'S
INFLUENCE—ENTRANCE AT ETON.

ABOUT the middle of the last century the rectory of
Humber, in Herefordshire, was held by the Rev.
James Hodgson.

Born towards the close of the reign of Queen
Anne, in the year 1711, he received his early education at the school of Hawkshead, in the Lake District,
in Lancashire, at that time a school of considerable
importance, at which the poet Wordsworth was subsequently educated. Ordained to the curacy of
Humber, he served that parish for many years as
curate before he was presented to its rectory by King
George III. His sound theological learning, and the

earnest piety of his disposition, are amply attested by the many sensible and practical sermons which he left; and for the twenty years during which he held the living he appears to have led the useful, unobtrusive life of a country clergyman, in the faithful discharge of his parochial duties, and in quiet intercourse with the families in the neighbourhood. About the year 1735 he married Elizabeth, daughter of the Rev. Henry Vaughan, vicar of the neighbouring parish of Leominster.

The general question of hereditary influences is perhaps more fitted for the discussion of the genealogist than of the biographer; but when characteristic traits are distinctly noticeable in successive generations of a family, some mention of them in a biography cannot be considered to be foreign to its subject and purpose. The intense love of poetry which exercised so strong an influence upon the character of Francis Hodgson, the subject of the present memoir, does not appear to have been inherited from his father or grandfather, although both exhibited a fondness for classical compositions in prose and verse. But there is more reason to suppose that the poetic faculty may have descended to him from the family of Vaughans into which his grandfather married. It may not therefore be considered altogether irrelevant or uninteresting to mention briefly what is known of this talented family.

In the short biographical sketch appended to the poems of Henry Vaughan, the Silurist,[1] edited by the Rev. H. F. Lyte, some account is given of its origin. We there read that

The poet Vaughan was descended from one of the most ancient and respectable families of the Principality, deducing its pedigree from the ancient kings of that country. Two of his ancestors, Sir Roger Vaughan and Sir David Gam, lost their lives at the battle of Agincourt. His great-grandmother was Lady Frances Somerset, daughter of Thomas Somerset, third son of Henry, Earl of Worcester ; and the possessions of the Vaughan family were very extensive, both in Brecknockshire and other parts of Wales. The chief family residence was the castle of Tretower, in the parish of Cwmdû, and when it was dismantled, Skethrock or Scethrog, in the same neighbourhood. At this latter place Shakspeare is said to have paid a visit to one of the family, and his commentator, Malone, thinks that it was perhaps there that he picked up the

---

[1] That part of the Welsh border in which the Vaughans lived was called Siluria.

word 'Puck,' concerning the origin of which some of his critics have been much puzzled. 'Pooky,' in Welsh, signifies a goblin, and near Skethrog exists a valley Cwm-Pooky, the goblin's vale, which belonged to the Vaughans, and which a tradition, still extant, states to have been a favourite resort of some distinguished bard, who had once visited that neighbourhood.   From Tretower Henry Vaughan's grandfather migrated to Newton in the parish of Llansainfread, and there, in 1621, the poet was born.

His life presents a pleasing picture of pious learning and loyal devotion to the cause of his king ; and his poetry which is much in the style of George Herbert, although of a more refined character throughout, is replete with original sentiments clothed in quaint but vigorous language.

It appears probable that the property of the Vaughans was confiscated at the period of the Commonwealth, sharing the fate which was common to that of many other adherents of the Royal Cause.   Be this as it may, we find as a fact that in the next generation but one, the vicarage of Leominster, in the same county, was held by the Rev. Henry Vaughan. The father of the vicar is known to have been Dr.

William Vaughan, probably the son or nephew of the poet, a physician at Leyden, and subsequently in practice in London and at the court of Queen Mary, wife of William III., whom he appears to have previously attended and to have accompanied to England. In 1676 he married Miss Newton, sister of Sir Henry Newton, who was employed by Queen Anne as envoy-extraordinary to the great Duke of Tuscany, and to the republic of Genoa. Sir Henry Newton married a Manning, and his two daughters, Mary and Catherine, married respectively Henry Rodney, the father of the distinguished admiral Lord Rodney, and Lord Aubrey Beauclerk, youngest son of the first Duke of St. Albans. With the latter lady, who was his first cousin, Henry Vaughan, vicar of Leominster, had much interesting correspondence. In one of her letters she begs him to write an epitaph on her father, Sir Henry Newton, 'whose life,' she adds, 'a gentleman is writing at Gottingen; who writes the life I know not, nor where Gottingen is at this present.' The MS. copy of this epitaph by Henry Vaughan is extant, and is a curious specimen of the lapidary Latin of the period. An English translation is appended to it, at the close of which its readers are reminded that

On his return from Genoa (having discharged his high

trust with successful fidelity) he was, by Her Majesty's Royal munificence, appointed Master of St. Catharine's Hospital. In the beginning of the reign of King George I. he was made judge of the High Court of Admiralty as a proof of the high esteem that wise prince had of his knowledge and integrity. A lover he was of good men and by them beloved, but in an especial manner dear to the renowned Lord Somers, Chancellor of England ; whose friendship was an honour he worthily accounted among the greatest which he enjoyed. In the execution of his office whilst he was doing his duty, he died. His most loving wife, mortally wounded with the same stroke, scarcely surviving, sighed away her breath, faithful companion of his life and death.

Henry Vaughan was acquainted with Dean Swift, and appears to have been a cultivated and agreeable person. His sermons are sensible and pointed, and his tenure of the vicarage was distinguished by energy and prudence, to which ample testimony is borne by the ' History of Leominster,' lately republished. He was vicar nearly forty years. During his incumbency many important improvements were made in the beautiful parish church, now undergoing restoration by

Sir Gilbert Scott. The adorning of the altar by Mr. Locke in 1725, the augmentation of the benefice in 1730 by the collection of £400, half paid by the parishioners and half by Queen Anne's Bounty; the grants given by the vestry for the daily reading of the prayers; the reflooring and levelling of the north aisle in 1734; the erection of the first organ after the fire in 1737; the increase and recasting of the bells in 1756: all these various proceedings speak of a good understanding between himself and his parishioners, and are memorials of his work and usefulness. They are, moreover, interesting as evidences of religious earnestness at a period which it is the fashion of the present day to decry as altogether barren of ecclesiastical energy, and equally devoid of all zeal and practical improvement in matters connected with Church work and discipline.

The vicar died in 1762 aged 75, and was buried by his son-in-law, the Rev. James Hodgson, rector of Humber, in *woollen*, pursuant to the statute in that case made and provided. This statute, which was repealed in the reign of George III., was passed in 1678 for the encouragement of the woollen trades. He had two sons, of one of which there remains a copy of poems in manuscript under the title ' Poematum Miscellaneorum Eruditissimi Domini Gulielmi

Vaughan ex oppido Leominstriæ Editio novissima, 1737.' Their style is not unlike that of Henry Vaughan, the Swan of the Usk, of whom mention has been made above, and the poetry comprises a curious combination of classical and religious subjects, pastoral poems and love songs being strangely intermingled with arguments against atheism such as, it is to be feared, a modern sceptic would scarcely consider convincing. Several of these poems are addressed to the writer's sister, Mrs. Hodgson.

Henry Vaughan, the favourite physician of George IV., who, on being created a baronet, assumed the arms and surname of Sir Charles Halford, whose widow he married; Sir John Vaughan, judge of the Common Pleas; Dr. Peter Vaughan, Dean of Chester; and Sir Charles Vaughan, envoy-extraordinary to the United States, were great-grandsons of the vicar of Leominster; and Dr. Vaughan, the present master of the Temple, is his great-great-grandson.

James, the son of James and Elizabeth Hodgson (née Vaughan), was educated at Charterhouse under Dr. Crusius, and matriculated at Christ Church, Oxford, in 1766, where he took the usual degrees. The expenses for taking an M.A. degree a hundred years ago may be amusingly compared with those of the present day.

	£	s.	d.
For a Liceat to do Quodlibets . .	0	0	6
For Six Wall-Lectures	0	3	0
For a Liceat to do Augustines . . .	0	14	0
For Ditto to Declamations	0	7	6
For Ditto to Examination	0	10	0
For the use of Schools and Hoods . . .	0	4	0
To Proctor's Men	0	2	0
To Dispensations—Regency Degree . .	7	9	0
To the Xt. Ch: Library	0	18	0
To the Presenter	0	10	6
To the Common Room	0	6	8
To Gown	1	18	0
To Hood	1	10	0
To Cap	0	7	6
To Scout for Attendance	0	5	0
	£15	5	2

In 1771, James Hodgson the younger was
ordained deacon as curate to his father's church of
Humber, in the rectory of which he subsequently
succeeded his father. Two years later he took priest's
orders, and, being a sound scholar and noted for impressive eloquence in the pulpit, he had not long to
wait for preferment. In 1774, through the influence of
the first Lord Liverpool, who was also a Carthusian,
he was appointed by the Archbishop of Canterbury
to the mastership of the school and hospital founded
by Archbishop Whitgift at Croydon, to which was

attached the neighbouring rectory of Keston.   In the following year he married Jane, daughter of the Rev. Richard Coke of Lower Moor, in his native county of Herefordshire, and on November 16, 1781, his second son, Francis, was born at Croydon.

The tender affection which Francis Hodgson ever entertained towards his mother and her family evidently exercised a strong influence upon his disposition, and hereditary Coke characteristics were manifested in many traits of his character.   A memoir of his life would therefore be incomplete without some brief notice of this ancient, and, in the case of several of its members, distinguished family. Further particulars which had been written for this memoir have been anticipated by the 'Life of Lord Melbourne,' whose descent from the Cokes in the female line was precisely similar to that of Francis Hodgson.

Originally settled in Derbyshire, the Cokes were located about its borders from the time of the Norman Conquest.   In the 'History of Melbourne' in that county it is stated that the first member of the family actually resident within the limits of Derbyshire was one Robert Coke, who established himself at Trusley in the reign of Edward II.   His descendants for some centuries after this were content to enjoy their position as lords of the land, ambitious only to add lustre to the good name which the family had held from the remotest antiquity, and to pursue the quiet yet useful lives of English country gentlemen. It is probable that the Norfolk Cokes, to which the Great Chief-Justice Sir Edward Coke belonged (of whom, notwithstanding his many faults, no less an authority than Lord Bacon has said that 'Without him the law had been like a ship without ballast'), and from whom the earls of Leicester are lineally descended, were a branch of this family. About 1570 Richard Coke of Trusley married Mary Sacheverell, who inherited from her father considerable possessions in Nottinghamshire. Their joint fortune enabled them to acquire possession of Melbourne Castle in South Derbyshire, originally part of the royal demesne, and annexed by King John, by a strange caprice of patronage, to the see of Carlisle, as an episcopal residence. Their eldest son, Sir Francis Coke, married a daughter of the celebrated Denzil, Lord Holles; Sir John Coke, his brother, became Secretary of State to Charles I; while a third son, George, obtained the see of Bristol and afterwards that of Hereford. Sir John Coke was a fellow of Trinity College, Cambridge, in 1584, and was elected to the professorship of rhetoric in that University,[1] in which employment he so distinguished himself by his ingenious and critical lectures, that rhetoric seemed to be not so much an art to him as his nature. Then after travelling beyond the seas for some time and returning rich in languages, remarks, and experience, he retired into the country as a private gentleman until he was more than fifty years of age, when, 'upon some reputation he had for industry and diligence, he was called to a painful employment in the navy, which he discharged well, and was made secretary thereof.' He was Secretary of State for about twenty years, representing his University in Parliament; and Lord Clarendon, who had a strong prejudice against him, is obliged to confess that the secretary had gotten Latin learning enough,' and there are evidences still extant to prove that he was a statesman of no mean capabilities; prudent, thoughtful, honourable, and endowed with a cultivated taste and polished mind.

The 'History of Melbourne' gives a picturesque account of the ancient art of falconry, to which the secretary and his son and daughter were particularly attached. They kept several 'castes' of falcons, and in their quaint letters make many allusions to hawks and hawking. Sir John the younger, who was

---

[1] Clarendon's *History of the Rebellion.*

knighted during his father's lifetime, sat in the Long Parliament, and was one of the judges on Strafford's trial, writes humorously :

Mr. Harpur, son of Sir John Harpur of Calke, comes often hither (to Melbourne), pretending to see my hawks fly, but in reality to see my sister.

George Coke, brother to the secretary, was made Bishop of Bristol in 1632, and translated to Hereford in 1636. He was one of those bishops who signed the petition and protestation to Charles I. and the House of Lords against any laws which had been passed during their enforced and violent absence from the House ; and upon the accusation of high treason by the Commons, he was, with the other subscribers, committed to the Tower of London, where they remained until the bill for putting them into the House was passed, which was not until many months after.[1] The committee of Hereford confiscated his estates in the parish of Eardisley, and he was dependent upon his relations for maintenance. Walker, in his ' Sufferings of the Clergy,' says that this hard usage hastened his death, which happened in 1646; though Lloyd says that he bore his sufferings with admirable calmness and serenity, and adds that he

[1] Burke's *Commoners of England.*

was a pious and learned man. Lord Clarendon also describes him as meek, grave, and quiet, and much beloved by those who were subject to his jurisdiction.

The bishop died in 1646, and was buried in Eardisley Church. In Hereford Cathedral a handsome cenotaph was raised to his memory, which has lately been restored by some of his descendants. In the inscription on this cenotaph we are told that he ennobled his generous birth with every instance of virtue worthy of his ancestors ; and though every allowance must be made for the unchastened spirit of the Restoration, in which, as has been justly observed, the inscription was written, there can be but little doubt that he was a person of distinguished learning, of great firmness and discretion, and of a singular piety.

From Secretary Coke was descended the Right Honourable Thomas Coke, Vice-Chamberlain to Queen Anne, who married, first, a daughter of Lord Chesterfield ; afterwards, Miss Hale, a maid of honour to the Queen, remarkable for her beauty and accomplishments. She appears to have been a favourite with the Duchess of Marlborough, who describes her as ' a verie pretty young woman, and of a verie good family.' Swift says, in his Journal to Stella :

Mr. Coke, the Vice-Chamberlain, made me a long

visit this morning, but the toast, his lady, was
unfortunately engaged to Lady Sutherland. She
was also on terms of friendship with the poet Gay.
Lord Chesterfield, writing to his daughter, Lady
Mary Coke, complains of his own son, Wootton
Stanhope, and wishes that he was like her husband,
Mr. Coke, and adds: 'If in his place I had a son
like your husband, I should have gone out of the
world with the satisfaction of believing that I had
left one behind me who would make one of the
greatest men in England.' Mr. Coke's society was
much sought by the wits and fine gentlemen of the
day. With Lord Bolingbroke, particularly, he was
on terms of the greatest intimacy ; with the great
Duke and Duchess of Marlborough he was well
acquainted, and is said to have been the original of
Pope's Sir Plume in the 'Rape of the Lock.'

Charlotte Coke, daughter of the Vice-Chamberlain, in 1755 married Sir Matthew Lamb, and (her
brother dying without issue) succeeded to Melbourne
Castle, which thus became the property of her husband's family, and gave his title to her son, the first
Lord Melbourne, the father of the great Prime
Minister.

The wife of the Rev. James Hodgson was descended in the direct male line from the Bishop of Hereford. She died at the early age of thirty-six, and her son, Francis, cherished her memory with affectionate reverence to the last years of his life. Her husband has left a touching tribute to her worth, written soon after her death, which gives some idea of the pure maternal influences which, doubtless, had no slight share in developing the gentle and deeply religious temperament of her son.

She was naturally disposed to be grave and serious in her manners, and even in youth had none of that trifling levity which is so common in the generality of young people. . . . Ever to be honoured as well as loved, she had such a gentleness, such a graceful composure in all she said and did, such a desire to oblige, such a modest attention to her friends, as made her company more delightful than I can now express. Fond of retirement, her sole study was my happiness and welfare, and that of her children and family. Her steady perseverance in what her strong good sense showed her was right, her scorn of whatever was extravagant, mean, or base, her superiority to all that was vain or frivolous, the decided preference which she gave to what was solid and useful to all that was showy and unnecessary, were excellencies that place her above most married women. But as a mother she shone with still brighter lustre. It was with her a most sacred duty to attend to every circumstance that was nearly or remotely connected with the health and improvement of her children ; she never, in any one instance, nor in the most trying situations, remitted in the smallest degree that love and anxious care she felt for them. Sleep, and food, and friends, and health, all were sacrificed to them. She lived for them, and her end was probably accelerated by her unwearied solicitude for their good. Her religious principles, formed by education, were confirmed by reflection and the daily practice of prayer and reading the Scriptures, which were her chief delight. Her sincere faith in the Gospel supported her alike in sorrows and sickness, and, speaking peace at the last, enabled her to meet her fate with the same composed resignation which she possessed in all her life.

Francis Hodgson himself always attributed his intense fondness for Holy Scripture to his early religious training and to the daily reading of the Psalms at his mother's knee. He felt her loss keenly for many years after her death, which occurred when he was quite young. His elementary classical education was conducted by his father, of whom he writes in terms of deep gratitude and affection ; and in July 1794 he was sent to Eton, passed his examination for college at that election, and so first became a member of that great foundation, over which, after the lapse of nearly half a century, he was destined to preside as Provost.

CHAPTER II.

ETON—CAMBRIDGE—CHOICE OF A PROFESSION—
EARLY FRIENDSHIPS.

1794—1807.

OF Eton life at the end of the last and beginning of
the present century there is no very exact record.
Although the discomforts of Long Chamber, the
abuse of the fagging system, and the other various
defects of diet, discipline, and accommodation which
have so often and so feelingly been described by those
who were subjected to them, had not, perhaps, at
this period, reached their height, yet the condition of
the collegers was certainly not such as Henry VI.
intended it to be, and Hodgson, from boyhood until
the end of his life, always entertained earnest wishes
for its improvement. How these wishes were even-
tually fulfilled the account of his Provostship will show.

Mr. John Keate, afterwards the renowned Head
Master Dr. Keate, was Hodgson's tutor at Eton, and
maintained a cordial friendship with him throughout

his life. When in 1840 it was suggested to Hodgson that he should stand for the Provostship, he refused to do so until he had ascertained that his old friend and tutor had ceased to desire it.

Among his Eton contemporaries were many boys who were subsequently distinguished in Church and State. William Lamb, afterwards the great Lord Melbourne, John Bird Sumner, Archbishop of Canterbury, Lancelot Shadwell, the Vice-Chancellor, George Thackeray, Provost of King's College, Cambridge, Henry Drury, the distinguished Harrow Master, were, by a few years, his seniors at Eton; while among his juniors were Scrope Davies and Charles Skinner Matthews, of both of whom Byron has left an interesting account, John Lonsdale, Bishop of Lichfield, Benjamin Heath Drury, the witty and original Eton Master, and Gally Knight, the antiquary and writer upon art. With all of these Hodgson was more or less intimate in after years; while with Edward Craven Hawtrey, who was several years younger, he subsequently formed a warm friendship which he maintained until the end of his life.

At Eton his love of learning was fully indulged, and he wandered widely over the fields of French and English literature without, in any measure, sacrificing that which, at the period of which we are speaking, was considered the one essential of an Eton education, classical scholarship, elegant as well as accurate. A manuscript copy of his 'Ludi Juveniles,' written in 1798, contains many Greek and Latin verses of a very high order of merit, while the soundness and solidity of his classical knowledge is amply attested by several terse and vigorous Latin essays. In 1799 he was elected to a scholarship at King's College, Cambridge, where he took the usual degrees, being excluded from public classical competition by the prejudicial restrictions then imposed upon Kingsmen. His own description of his college at this period expresses forcibly how detrimental such restrictions were to the best interests of University education.

Our having all been at the same school certainly deadened emulation by placing us in that rank at Cambridge in which we relatively stood at Eton. Neither had we any public honours to contend for ; and ambition thus too often expired in indolence.

The force of this observation is not materially affected by the fact that King's is pre-eminent among colleges for the number of its distinguished 'alumni.' The excellence of the Eton education which all Kingsmen had previously enjoyed was at all times exceptional, and the impossibility of gaining University distinction may have acted as an incentive to increased exertion in the great contest of life, upon those ardent spirits who did not accept the honours which their Alma Mater can bestow as the highest summit of human ambition. One of the necessary evils of the competitive system is undoubtedly to be found in the fact that in many cases it affixes too final and conclusive an estimate of a young man's powers. If in his own opinion, as well as in that of his contemporaries, a youth of twenty-two or twenty-three leaves college with the brand of a second or third class upon him, there is certainly danger, unless his temperament is unusually sanguine, that he should accept the examiner's decision as final. It may be argued with undoubted truth that real merit will make its way against all such temporary obstacles; but when we consider the many circumstances which may contribute to unmerited failure —such, for instance, as illness at the times of the examinations, the almost irresistible influences of a fast and noisy college, the want of pecuniary means to complete the full University career, too often necessitating the work of tuition in vacations in order to eke out a scanty income—we cannot but feel the utter unfairness of which many narrow-minded persons are guilty when they accept that certificate as final which in reality merely announces what a man has done at a certain period of his life, and gives no conclusive clue whatever to what he can do.

One special advantage may, moreover, be mentioned in connection with the absence of competitive examinations. Not being required to be constantly engaged in preparation of a special character, a naturally studious youth had leisure for far more extensive reading than would otherwise have been possible, and perhaps was sufficiently compensated for the loss of University prizes by the acquirement of a wider and more general stock of knowledge.

But notwithstanding the impossibility of public competition, Francis Hodgson's abilities were not overlooked, and by those of his contemporaries who were most competent to judge he was considered as one of the best classical scholars of his time at Cambridge.

His vacations were spent chiefly at Croydon, and at Lower Moor in Herefordshire, the home of his mother's kindred, the Cokes; and his home studies, carried on under his father's supervision, were participated in by a young nobleman, who was destined to attain to the highest eminence. Two of his father's pupils at this time were sons of a brother-Carthusian the first Lord Liverpool. The eldest of these brothers, then Lord Hawkesbury, became afterwards, as second Lord Liverpool, one of the most illustrious Prime Ministers who ever presided over the destinies of this country. With him Mr. Hodgson read, among other subjects, Locke's two great works on 'The Conduct of the Understanding' and 'The Essay on the Human Understanding;' and it was, doubtless, during these early holiday readings that Francis Hodgson imbibed that taste for metaphysical studies which subsequently led to his being appointed to the lectureship on metaphysics in his college. With the younger brother,[1] Cecil Jenkinson, who was a few years his junior, Hodgson formed a warm boyish friendship, and in their studies and amusements they appear to have derived mutual satisfaction from one another's society. The following are some of the authors which are recorded as having been among those which they read together :—Plato, Demosthenes, Homer, Cicero (with ' Middleton's Life '), Sir W. Raleigh's ' Persian History,' Bacon on ' The Advancement of Learning.' Lord Liverpool's views on his son's education, though full of sound sense and judgment, may, doubtless, be thought peculiar in the present day. But they are interesting as an illustration of the idea of a liberal education entertained by an

---

[1] Afterwards third Lord Liverpool.

intelligent nobleman at the commencement of the present century.

GREEK.

To read Herodotus till Cecil appears tired of it. Then to read Xenophon's 'Anabasis,' and then to read Plato's 'Phædo' and some of his other dialogues. Whenever he has finished these, which will probably be in the course of the year, then to resume Homer, and to read about eight more books, as Mr. Hall says the Westminster scholars always read in the whole twelve books before they come to Christ Church, and never more.

LATIN.

To begin with reading the 'Third Decad of Livy,' or some part of Cicero's works, or to take them occasionally, one after the other. Of Cicero's works Lord L. doubts whether Cecil had not better read the 'Quæstiones Academicæ;' and he is of opinion that he should continue to read one or other of these books till the beginning of the summer, when he may read two of the 'Satires' of Juvenal—that is, those translated by Johnson—and one of the best 'Satires' of Persius. These will lead him to read with effect Horace's 'Epistles and

Satires;' his understanding will by that time probably be equal fully to comprehend the sense and wit of Horace's writings, and he will be able to compare the different characters of the three Roman satirists. Lord Liverpool wishes that Cecil's reading in Latin with Mr. Hodgson may conclude with a book or two of Tacitus; but this should be his last business. Any intermediate time may be filled up with reading again Virgil's 'Georgics,' some of Martial's best 'Epigrams,' or a play or two of Terence, or perhaps a book of Claudian.

ENGLISH.

Cecil has read so many English books that Lord L. is at a loss to recommend what book he should read after he has finished Sir Walter Raleigh's History. He has lent him Lord Molesworth's account of 'The Revolution in Denmark,' and an old 'History of the Czar Peter the First.' Lord Molesworth's book is an excellent one, and he wishes him to read this soon, because he may then read Vertot's 'Revolutions of Sweden,' which contains a short but excellent account of the history of that country to the death of the first Gustavus, and this book is truly classical. He should then

read the life of Gustavus Adolphus, King of
Sweden, who, in conjunction with Cardinal Riche-
lieu, broke the power of the House of Austria.
He may then read Voltaire's 'Charles XII.,' who
destroyed the power of the Swedish monarchy by
his mad conceits. This is an amusing book, but
not a good one. He may also read Vertot's
'Revolution of Portugal,' which is excellent, and
as amusing as any novel that ever was written.
Lord Liverpool will send him Cartesa's 'History
of Catharine II.,' which Lord H.[1] commends greatly,
and says it contains more information respecting
the Russian empire than any book he ever met
with. It is singular that Cecil hardly ever reads
either any English or French poetry. He has said
repeatedly to Lord L. that he ought to read these
books and that he is determined to read them,
though they give him no great pleasure ; and it is
observable that after he has begun any book of
this kind he generally lays it aside. It would not
be right to press him upon this point ; he will probably take these sorts of books up, at some future
period, when he can relish them ; but Lord L.
submits to Mr. Hodgson whether, when they are in
want of some English book to read together, they

[1] Lord Holland (?).

might not read Milton's 'Paradise Lost,' and perhaps Shakespeare's play of 'Othello,' which in point
of composition is the most correct of all his
plays.

MATHEMATICS.

Cecil, while he has been at home during these short
holidays, has applied himself to Algebra, and
appears to have made some progress in it and
begins to find it not difficult.   He should be left to
proceed in this branch of knowledge as his inclination may direct him.—In the foregoing plan Lord
L. has endeavoured to trace his general ideas, as it
will be some time now before he returns to Addiscombe.   He does not mean, however, that these
ideas should be pursued either in contradiction to
the judgment of Mr. Hodgson, or to any particular
inclinations which Cecil may occasionally disclose.
He is certain that the best way of instructing a
young man, with a view to eminence, is to suffer
him to pursue those studies for which he shows the
greatest inclination, and to which his talents are
more particularly fitted.

This plan was supplemented by a letter written
soon afterwards.

London : January 4, 1800.

Dear Sir,—I have thought much on the paper I gave
you respecting the future plan of Cecil's education.
I wrote it in a great hurry, and traced out in
general what occurred to me. I wish only that
such parts of it may be executed, as may appear to
you to be practicable, and may not, from its labour,
give any disgust to my son ; my great object, however, is that as long as he is under your tuition, he
should direct his principal attention to the Greek
and Latin languages. His general reading both in
English and French has been so very extensive,
and so far exceeds what has usually been read by a
person of his age, that any further progress therein
ought to give way to his improvement in the two
learned languages. These he can only learn at
present. The former he may resume at any time,
and I have no doubt that his natural disposition
will incline him to resume it. I have already
observed, in the paper I gave you, that as his pursuit in mathematics is a favourite object of his own,
he should be left to proceed in that at leisure times
as his inclination may direct him. I am sorry to
give you this trouble, but I have thought it right in
this manner freely to explain myself, as you must
be sensible how much I have this object at heart,

and how much I am interested in my son's future welfare. I beg my best compliments to Mrs. Hodgson, and I am, my dear sir, with great regard,

Your faithful, humble servant,

LIVERPOOL.

A boyish letter from the subject of this anxious father's solicitude to his friend Francis Hodgson, at Cambridge, presents, in its light-hearted simplicity, an amusing contrast.

My dear Frank,—I must make you a great many apologies for not having written before, which I assure you I have not had time to do. We have gone on in the old way since I saw you, and have finished the 'Life of Agricola' and the third book of Xenophon's 'Anabasis.' I was glad to hear you were so fortunate as to meet with some of your friends in the stage-coach in which you returned to Cambridge. I hope you do not find the college very empty and dull. I have, since you left Croydon, read that novel you were so much pleased with, 'Castle St. Donats.' I like it very much, except the last volume. Is Bacon returned to college? if he is, pray remember me to him. Your father has begun to make preparations for his departure hence; we next week remove to the dining-room, and prosecute our studies there, as the library is to be totally gutted. Pray write to me soon and let me know how 'Josephus' goes on, which Mr. H. informs me you have begun. I have been but once a-shooting since I saw you; I shot one snipe, the first I ever killed in my life. Have you been after the hounds lately?

I am, dear Frank,
Yours sincerely,
C. JENKINSON.

The departure alluded to in this letter refers to Mr. Hodgson's removal to Barwick-in-Elmet, near Leeds, a valuable Yorkshire living which Lord Liverpool's influence had procured for him from the Chancellor. This removal, although it brought with it an increase of fortune, must, for many reasons, have been a source of regret. The neighbourhood of Croydon at this period was by no means devoid of interest. From 1793 to 1802 the vicarage was held by the Rev. John Ireland, afterwards the distinguished Dean of Westminster, and founder of the Greek scholarship at Oxford which bears his name; and his old friend and schoolfellow William Gifford, author of the 'Baviad' and 'Mæviad,' and editor of the 'Quarterly

Review,' was a frequent visitor at the vicarage. Both of these eminent scholars and men of letters were acquainted with Francis Hodgson in his youth and early manhood, and took a kindly and considerate interest in his career.

About the year 1800 Louis Philippe paid a visit to Addiscombe, and young Hodgson had the honour of meeting him—an honour which was renewed under somewhat different circumstances forty years afterwards, at Windsor Castle.

At Cambridge several valuable friendships were added to those already formed at Eton and Croydon. Thomas Denman, the future Chief Justice, and John Herman Merivale, were undergraduates at St. John's; Robert Bland, editor of the 'Anthology,' was at Pembroke ; Harry Drury was a fellow of King's. With all of these Hodgson formed affectionate intimacies, which were only terminated by death. A kind of club was founded for the promotion of good fellowship and sociability ; letters were constantly interchanged in prose and verse, on subjects of religion, politics, philosophy, classical and modern literature ; and the warmest interest was maintained by these kindred spirits in their mutual advancement and success. About the year 1801 Harry Drury was appointed to a classical mastership at Harrow, and

Hodgson writes to him from Hawtrey's [1] rooms at King's :—

Dear Drury,—I am heartily glad to hear that you have recovered your health so far as to go into school. Bethell [2] reports this, and your brother [3] tells me you hoped to do so when you last wrote to him. I hope you are now in no danger of a relapse, and have dismissed your glomy ideas as to retaining an enemy within:

> Musis amicus tristitiam et metus
> Tradas severis in caput hostium
> Portare curis.

I promised you last night the conclusion of my long strain of nonsense.

Here follow some half-humorous, half-serious lines on matters of mutual interest, a few of which may be quoted as an amusing comment on public school manners and customs of the period, and as proving the writer's early desire for their amendment.

> Yes, I could wish our rich and noble fools
>   Restrain'd in vices and curtail'd in dress ;
> Much could I wish that *all* our public schools [4]
>   Were better managed or encouraged less.

---

[1] Afterwards Vicar of Broad Chalke, Wilts, and uncle to Provost Hawtrey.   [2] Fellow of Eton.

[3] Benjamin Drury, Master at Eton. [4] Except Harrow, of course.—F. H

> If learning's stores were open to the mind,
> If emulation woke the dormant flame,
> If labour nerved us, ere we simply dined,
> And weekly washings exercised my dame.
> If holy worship claim'd respectful awe,
> If good example taught the young to pray,
> If Decency did not proceed from Law,
> Nor discipline usurp the Sabbath Day.

You shall have no more original farrago for some time. But now you have got into school again, I shall hope to hear oftener from you; perhaps you'll say you are more engaged, but I know at night you can find time to send me some poetry. I mean to begin the study of history from the Creation—old A. recommends Josephus. Is it not better to read in English what is not well done in Greek or Latin? Prettyman and Prideaux are surely preferable to Josephus and Dio Cassius. Dr. A. has written a plan of study, and says from Lipsius 'Triennii res est.' Now two years of my scholarship are over, and I don't think ten would suffice to get through the doctor's plan. It was sent from Croydon to a young nobleman here many years ago. He never looked into it, and I must confess it frightens me. Enough of Mr. Erskine's monosyllable here, you'll say. Is not *Wegotism* a good name for that style, which, in-

stead of 'Ego et mea,' pesters you with 'nos nos-
traque' when used by only one author? B. is very
correct, and as good-natured and stupid as ever.
Adieu, and believe me yours sincerely,

F. H.

P.S. Pray send me your translations from
Statius. I don't mind double or even treble letters.

When single letters cost a shilling this was a
stronger proof of friendship than it might be considered in the present day.

Having taken his degree, Hodgson obtained a
private tutorship to the sons of Lady Ann Lambton,
who had been married a second time to Mr. Wynd-
ham. The eldest of these pupils was afterwards
created Earl of Durham, and attained considerable
eminence as Governor-General of British North
America. His sister married Byron's relative, Major
Howard, who fell at Waterloo, and to whom so
touching an allusion is made in the Third Canto of
'Childe Harold.'

This charge continued three years, and Hodgson
appears to have felt the restraint extremely irksome,
and to have constantly chafed at the drudgery of
'gerund-grinding,' although he speaks with gratitude
of the kindness and consideration which he experi-

enced. His genial and affectionate nature longed for the society of his friends, and found its chief consolation in constant correspondence. It was about this time that he conceived the idea of writing a translation of 'Juvenal,' and this occupation also afforded considerable relief to a mind which was daily growing more and more melancholy while engaged in the tedious pursuits which were necessarily imposed upon it.

During a vacation spent in Devonshire he paid a visit to his friend's father, the former head master of Harrow, of whom Byron used to speak as the *dear* Drury, in contradistinction to his successor, whom he maliciously designated the *cheap* Butler, but whom he afterwards learned to estimate at his proper value. To Dr. Drury's kindly appreciation of youthful talent Hodgson bears testimony in a letter written from Exmouth to his friend at Harrow.

I am sitting in a room which looks immediately upon your father's house. There I have had a look at it. We returned from Cockwood[1] yesterday after a very pleasant stay of two days. It was to me quite a delightful break. On the Thursday Sir George Dallas, rather a quiz, but good-humoured and entertaining ; Mr. Blencowe, a most clever and gentlemanly old Etonian, who told many good

[1] Dr. Drury's.

stories which are for your future ear; Mr. Hoare, an interesting deaf person (quite unlike the Provost of King's [1]), your father and mother, Charles Nicholson, and I were of the party. On Friday morning I got up early and transcribed some parallel passages from Boileau, and some illustrations from Dio in the library. I have given your father the conclusion of my tenth Satire. He has been of considerable service to me with regard to accuracy in the former parts; and he very kindly took an interest in my notes, referred to Denon, Tacitus, Pausanias, &c. (but you had stolen the Strabo), and threw much light upon Ombites and Tentyrites and Memnon's statue. I congratulated him upon your success at Harrow. He said he hoped you would not build, and asked me if I did not think he had built enough for you at Cockwood. Upon the whole I had a most agreeable visit, and before I leave Exmouth shall certainly take advantage of his reinvitation and go and see him again.

This second visit elicited one of those rhyming epistles in which Hodgson and his friends were wont to communicate to one another their current fancies and feelings on subjects of mutual interest, and from

[1] Humphrey Sumner.

which a few extracts may be found interesting, not only from their natural ease and freshness but as specimens of a style of correspondence which has now long been obsolete.

The same to the same.

Clifton : Wednesday night.

Dear Drury,—We go to Chepstow to-morrow. On Sunday Mr. Merivale very kindly took us to Fordlands, &c., &c., a beautiful drive, and dined with us at Cockwood, where I slept, and went, next morning, to Bishop's Teignton, to see my uncle and aunt. On the road I made the following verses for you :—

> Alone, on horseback, from the wood of Cock,
>   To Dawlish town I took my early way,
> View'd the mild ocean from the lofty rock,
>   And felt the cooling breath of pleasant May.
> Now every field in smiling green array'd,
>   Puts forth the promise of the fruitful spring,
> The rising hedgerows shoot a deeper shade,
>   And joyous birds in flowery meadows sing.
> I too to friendship raise the glowing strain,
>   Warn'd by remembrance of my Father's home,
> In careless dreams shake off my servile chain,
>   And far to Harrow's verdant upland roam.
> Oh soon exulting o'er the much-loved hill,
>   By Freedom led thy happy friend shall run,
> See the proud aspens lift their honours still,
>   And the vale glittering with the genial sun.

And soon o'er Uxbridge' rabbit-cover'd moor
   Shall stumbling Lightfoot[1] show his speckled gray,
We'll haste delighted to our Osborne's door,
   And spend with him a memorable day.
Haply at times, when eve remits your toil,
   We'll range together o'er the dewy field,
And press with eager step the turfy soil,
   On thy light down, O distant Harrow weald.
And then, should Fancy with seductive eye
   Onward to Stanmore's environs allure,
Should Reservoir excite a tender sigh,
   This faithful heart shall offer Friendship's cure.
Back to their cottage shall the brothers go,
   And sit conversing o'er the social board,
Share equal portions of imparted woe,
   And share the joy poetic dreams afford.

Lower Moor :[2] June 2.

Dear Drury,—All intermediate accounts must be deferred till we meet. Suffice it to say now that I have found, as ever from childhood, an affectionate reception here. We leave the place on Saturday, I believe, and before the end of the next week, perhaps, we may meet. But now consider in secret this important question, that you may be able to decide upon your friend's future prospects in life. Denman has offered me a private tutorship to the son of a Mr. Oswald of Ayrshire, a very rich man,

---

[1] A favourite horse.   [2] The Rev. Francis Coke's.

the boy going to Eton. But I cannot conquer my
aversion to private tutorships. The Law all my
friends set their faces against. Give me your
advice, when we meet.   F. H.

Another letter written in a similar strain of
anxious uncertainty concludes with a few somewhat
desponding lines in anticipation of the flight of time.

> Then age a gloom on all our club shall throw,
> And sterner wisdom sit on Denman's brow ;
> Vocal no more, shall Bland's high spirits fall,
> And Walford's treble voice be none at all.
> Then Nature's sons shall learn dishonest art,
> And e'en my Merivale be hard of heart.
> O long protracted be the fatal day,
> That steals, unpitying, all our joys away,
> The joke, the gybe, the jeer, that only find
> A moment's meaning in the kindred mind.

John Herman Merivale, alluded to in these lines,
fully deserved the implied compliment. A kinder-
hearted man, or one more unselfishly interested in
his friend's welfare, never breathed. Hearing that
Hodgson was dissatisfied and depressed by his present
circumstances, he wrote the following cheerful effusion :—

Dear Hodgson,—In the letter which Bland and I,
desultorily as usual, composed at the half-way

house last Saturday I said nothing on the subject
of yours which I had just then received—because
of course I said not a word to him about it. But
your melancholy strains gave me much room for
reflection both going and coming; and reflection
presented itself in a poetical form. Such as my
thoughts were, take them.

Life is not made to flow in smooth delight,
   Nor to be lost in unavailing sorrow ;
It is a chequer'd scene of dark and light,
   The clouds scarce form'd to-day may burst to-morrow.
It is for action given, for mental force,
   For deeds of energetic hardihood ;
There is no time for wailing and remorse,
   There is no room for dreary solitude.
There is no day doth pass but teems with fate,
   No fleeting hour but alteration brings ;
O'er this our perishable mortal state
   Variety for ever waves her wings.
Vain is the lay, tho' couch'd in sacred writ,
   That Israel's fastidious monarch sung,
Tho' since usurp'd by many an idle wit,
   By many a melancholy sophist's tongue.
Let not my 'Narva'[1] then of change complain,
   A change which governs our sublunar sphere ;
Nor waste in fond regret and listless pain
   The hours assign'd to generous action here.

[1] The name of a book which the friends had lately been reading,
and the title of which was transferred as a *soubriquet* to Hodgson.

The dreams of lawless youth, 'tis true, are fled,
  The glass brisk-circling and the jovial song,
The careless heart, the wild fantastic head
  That to the early burst of life belong ;—
All these are past ;—perhaps with them are flown
  Some cherished visions yet more closely twined,
Which soon Delusion fondly called her own,
  And Fate, unpitying, claims to be resign'd.
Perhaps the parting pang was worse than all
  That studious tyrants could invent of pain ;
Perhaps—but ah ! thy tortured thoughts recall,
  Think what remains in life,—awake again !
Has fickle Fancy fled ? Yet Friendship lives,
  And breathes a balm into the wounded heart.
Firm, faithful Friendship, which survives
  The storms of Hate, and never will depart.
Are youth's chimæras check'd ? Ambition glows
  With fiercer heat in our maturer age,
Honour is left—the foe to dull repose—
  And points a hard, but glorious pilgrimage.
And shall, my ' Narva,' such a soul as thine,
  So bright with genius, and in vigour warm,
Now, at the very prime of life, decline,
  Nor burst again through Fortune's partial storm ?
Perish the thought ! for nobler objects made—
  Let nobler resolutions fire thy soul ;
Call Honour, Virtue, Courage, to thy aid,
  And let warm Friendship still inspire the whole.

Did you write the review of Dermody ?[1] I was de-

---

[1] Thomas Dermody, a young Irish bard, whose principal poems
were 'The Battle of the Bards' and 'The Reform.' The review was
by Hodgson.

lighted with it. Edinburgh critics I have not read; but if they abuse the wretch Heaven have mercy on their black souls, say I. Write to me from the road, and   Believe me

Ever your most affectionate friend,

J. H. MERIVALE.

The attractions of London life for a young man appear not to have been lost upon Hodgson, from a description written by him a few years later.

It is impossible that anyone, who has not experienced the first captivation of London, for ardent spirits, high health, and lively fancy in youth, should fairly appreciate so dangerous a charm. It is not merely the more refined luxuries of the idle bachelor's life; not the new sights, nor even the immense superiority of intellectual resources, in which that wondrous city abounds, to a degree that makes the University seem perfectly Bæotian to an incompetent observer; it is not all this together; it is the delightful society of intelligent young men, on whom life has begun to open; and to whose *knowledge of the world* the school or college attainments of their younger acquaintance seems utter ignorance and stupidity. Alas! that *knowledge of the world.*

In 1806 he was appointed to a mastership at Eton, which he held for one year, and it was about this time that he first conceived the idea of translating Juvenal. Notwithstanding his innate dislike for teaching, this period of his life appears to have been sufficiently bright and joyous. He was extremely fond of all athletic exercises, for which by a robust and active frame he was eminently fitted, and was an excellent pedestrian. He more than once walked from Cambridge to London in a day, and thought nothing of a walk from London to Eton. He fully appreciated his many delightful friendships, and thoroughly enjoyed his holidays in Yorkshire, in his father's society, or with his Coke relations in Herefordshire. Of his father he speaks in terms of grateful affection.

I acquired much from his clear command of his own knowledge, and from a kindness of heart which one could not approach without improvement ; I truly honour his memory.

His own description of 1806–7, when he was first set free from the restraints necessarily imposed by a private tutorship, is an evidence of the happiness of his life at that time.

> How different now the paths of life appear'd,
>   Girt all the way with banks of varied flowers;
> Refresh'd by wit, by gay companions cheer'd,
>   How lightly flew the perishable hours !
> Musing, I sailed down Richmond's fabled stream;
>   Musing, I roam'd to Harrow's verdant height !
> The great Aquinian fill'd my glowing dream,
>   And Fame's imagined temple rose in sight.

His translation of Juvenal was begun and completed in about a year, during these solitary rambles and in a visit to Yorkshire.

The busy literary life which he was now leading is vividly described by Bland, who was then staying with him at Eton, in a letter [1] to Denman.

With the very little drop of ink remaining in the horn after the two epic poems, the six periodical papers, besides several epigrams, anagrams, and other things ending in 'grams,' and an infinite number of songs, sonnets, rebuses, pasquinades, and some things 'unattempted yet in prose or rhyme,' which Hodgson has written since breakfast up to this hour—twelve o'clock (not forgetting construing his boys and answering duns)—with that very little drop of ink remaining, I have to request of you, Denman, to order Merry's (Meri-

---

[1] Quoted by Sir Joseph Arnould in his *Memoir of Lord Denman*.

vale's) rooms to be opened, with sheets aired and a fire, on next Tuesday. . . . Hodgson is writing opposite to me in measured English, and has absolutely distanced me, who write *almost* in a desultory style.

It was about this time that the Bar was contemplated as a profession, and Denman's advice was asked on the subject. Denman knew enough of his friend's character to be convinced that such a friend to the Muses must lay aside all prospect of forensic preferment, and accordingly wrote the following characteristic letter of advice :—

My dear Hodgson,—You are mistaken in supposing that my communication of Mr. Oswald's proposal proceeded from a despair of your succeeding in the Law ; on the contrary, I think that, *if all other methods fail*, the Law may offer the highest opportunities of honour and emolument to talents such as yours. At the same time, if you ask my frank opinion which course is the most advisable, I cannot hesitate to recommend one trial more, even of the loathsome task of tutorship, before you enter on this hazardous profession. The expense it imposes is enormous, the labour unremitting, the advantages most doubtful and remote. . . .

You mention *reviewing* as a means of procuring money ; indeed it would be totally inconsistent with that complete devotion and abandonment to the Law which could alone give a probability of success. It is the duty of friendship to state these circumstances and offer this counsel, but if your aversion is unconquerable, remember that even the Law may be forced by *labor improbus* ; that Vevers's [1] chambers are open to receive you, and that it was his most ardent wish to have them occupied by you ; that it may be in my power and would be my delight to shorten your trouble and elucidate your views on legal subjects ; and that Merry and myself should rejoice to call you fellow-labourer in the same vineyard. Occasions do certainly occur in which general abilities are called into immediate action, and kept in constant employment ; if such occurred to you, no doubt your fame and fortunes would be fixed at once ; but that 'if' is a talisman which hardly any power of magic can command.

This letter seems much more calculated to perplex than enlighten you ; it is a picture of my own wavering and unsteady mind (!), which has poured out all its thoughts upon the subject as they arose.

---

[1] Denman's brother-in-law.

You will be sure that they are dictated by the warmest friendship and attachment, for God knows that (after my domestic feelings) no wish is so near my heart as that of seeing you independent and happy. I repeat the word *independent*, though it will not meet your ideas of tutorship, for I am sure it is fully as applicable to that position as his who lives on the smiles of attorneys.

Your sincere friend,

THOS. DENMAN.

The wisdom of this advice was at once recognised by its recipient, who henceforth abandoned all idea of the legal profession. His intense love of literature, and especially of poetry, would have, doubtless, constantly acted as an inducement to seek relief and mental relaxation in fresher fields than those which environ Lincoln's Inn; and the precarious prospect of advancement which attends even unceasing and undivided industry at the Bar, would have become proportionately smaller to one who looked upon it less as a profession than as a means of subsistence, and of more freely gratifying literary tastes and inclinations.

Denman's kind and timely counsel determined his future course, and from this year until the end of his life he devoted his time and thoughts exclusively to religion, education, and literature. He had already for some time been engaged in writing for reviews, a pursuit which he continued unremittingly for the next ten years, and during this period he also published many original poems and translations from the classics. Of the latter the most important was the translation of Juvenal, which will presently engage our attention, while the number and variety of the former entirely preclude their reproduction in this memoir. Even in the shape of samples or in the more fragmentary form of extracts, they would convey a most inadequate impression of their writer's power and versatility ; and those few verses which are quoted are merely intended to illustrate some passing incident, or to indicate the mental tone at the time of their composition.

The friendships already mentioned or implied in the correspondence were cherished with undiminished warmth, while fresh intimacies were formed of a no less interesting character. One, in particular, will demand a detailed description in several subsequent chapters. It was not later than the following year to that in which he returned to Eton as a master that Hodgson became the honoured friend and associate

of that brilliant but hapless youth of whom one of
England's greatest historians has recorded that he
was the most celebrated Englishman of the nineteenth century.

CHAPTER III.

TRANSLATION OF JUVENAL—CONTEMPORARY CRITIQUES.

1807-8.

THE translation of Juvenal, to which reference has already been made, appears to have been undertaken partly from admiration of the force and grandeur of the poetry, partly from a desire to make the great satirist more accessible to the majority of English readers, and thereby to apply his vigorous teaching to the vices and follies of the age.

It must be admitted that there never was a time when English morals more required the strong scourge of satire than the first two decades of the present century. The shameless intrigues of the Prince Regent were but a type of the prevailing immorality, and might well be compared to the excesses of those Roman emperors whose examples were polluting the Imperial city at the time when Juvenal wrote. London at the beginning of the nineteenth century of the Christian era was not much better than Rome in the first. The comparison must often have suggested itself to classical scholars.

The design and scope of this translation will most readily be understood by an epitome of the Introduction written by its author.

It is with the utmost diffidence (he writes) that I offer to the notice of the public a new translation of Juvenal. After the very spirited, although irregular, performance of Dryden and his coadjutors in the way of freer versions, and after the uncommonly faithful and meritorious work of Mr. Gifford, I am certainly called upon to say a few words in explanation of my own plan; and to state in what particulars my judgment has, perhaps erroneously, led me to believe that an improvement might be made upon the plan of my predecessors. That it is possible I still think, but am far from fancying that the design is here carried into execution.

After a few preliminary remarks upon the widely different construction of the Latin and English languages, especially in what relates to their poetical idiom, he goes on to say :—

It is a good fundamental maxim, that a translation

should be a complete and accurate copy of the original; that no addition or subtraction should be made; no image suppressed; no sentiment altered; that the very turn of particular phrases, if possible, but at any rate the style of thinking and expression, should be most faithfully preserved. There are three sets of readers: those who are unacquainted with the Latin; those who have when young read and enjoyed it, but have now an imperfect recollection; and those who will be at the pains of comparing original and translated poems. Every translator must wish ('speret idem, sudet multum frustraque laboret') the first class to rise from the perusal with a tolerably correct idea of the manner of the original; the second to have all their impressions brought fully to their minds, and often the very passages; the third to be quite astonished at finding that an imitation could be made at once so close and so spirited. But let me ask, has this fancied excellence been ever attained? has not one of the two contrary effects invariably prevailed? has not fidelity been sacrificed to versification, or poetry been excluded by a servile adherence to correctness? Pope and Cowper, in their respective translations of Homer, sufficiently answer the questions. But surely one must say,

'Mallem cum illo errare, quam cum hoc recte sentire.' An English poem in rhyme, whether translated or original, will never please, unless the verse be flowing, sweet, and simple, varied only by modifications of harmony, by dissimilar pauses, and a composed or hurried rhythm. But how are we to reconcile the sudden turns, the strong points, and striking contrasts of Juvenal with an equable, dignified, melodious cadence? Must we not lean more to another peculiarity of his character, that sweeping grandeur of declamation, that exalted style of poetical oratory, which are the chief properties of this sonorous writer? The English language compels diffuseness; a literal version is impossible; the Latin verse is nearly a fifth longer than our own; and the very nature of rhyme, forbidding one line to run into another, often obliges us to stretch phrases (for to contract them is seldom possible) very capriciously, for the benefit of the couplet. Then come the great curses of Gothicism, crowds of auxiliary verbs, and the the's, my's, thy's, em's, us's; which make our barbarous jargons, with their inharmonious monosyllables, bear the same resemblance to the ancient languages that a modern-built church, dotted with windows, bears to the graceful and commanding simplicity of a Grecian temple supported by pillars. Ad summam. The uniform imitation of language or style is, I hold, impossible; *i.e.* to write well in English, a translator of Juvenal must be defective in closeness of version, except where the author himself is easy and flowing in his manner. This, I contend, he generally is ; but to reconcile his occasional abruptness with English rhyme (the only species of our verse which can give effect to satire) is, it appears to me, a problem which can never be solved. The average of syllables in Latin hexameters is perhaps about fifteen ; as many as three dactyls usually occurring in a verse.[1] So that a person who attempted to translate Latin hexameters line for line into English heroic poetry, would have five extra syllables to cram into every verse ; which particular difficulty would be no slight one, not to mention the general conciseness of the Latin language (from the inflections of its nouns and verbs and various others causes), compared with the 'wild plenty' of the English. But the critic will here say 'Quorsum hæc ?' Nobody expects a literal translation of a Latin poet. It would be the attempt of a Procrustes ; fitting long and short alike to one inconvenient receptacle.

---

[1] Dryden rates the number as less ; Johnson rates it as above.

Well, but it was the attempt of Barten Holyday, that most learned of all the commentators upon Juvenal. The consequence of Holyday's passion for literal translation was, that he neither wrote sense nor poetry. As Dryden says, Holyday obtained his pedantic end ; namely, that of rendering his original line for line. Yet although such a plan as that of Holyday is evidently absurd, and both he, and the comparatively smooth Stapylton,[1] are obsolete as poetical translators of Juvenal, yet at the same time there is an opposite extreme of too great freedom in translation, of which, I own, I think Dryden and his associates have been guilty. It is perhaps needless to mention that Dryden himself only translated five out of the sixteen satires in the work that bears his name ; which were the first, third, sixth, tenth, and sixteenth. His assistants were numerous. . . . Charles Dryden, the poet's son, himself a poet, rendered the seventh. He had very good abilities ; but I think he betrays

---

[1] Johnson calls Stapylton smoother than Holyday. Take one of Stapylton's smooth lines :—

'Overwrit

O' th' sides, indorsed too, and not finish'd yet.' (*Sat.* i.)

But Stapylton is, upon the whole, very smooth indeed for the time in which he wrote. He is very nervous too ; and, I am sorry to say, Dryden owes many good lines to him, which he has not acknowledged.

his father's helping hand. Harvey, who I really think is the best of the band next to Dryden and Congreve, paraphrased the ninth very poetically. No one can doubt that Congreve would do anything well which he undertook. The Eleventh Satire was fortunate enough to engage his attention. His translation, faulty as it is in point of rhymes, surely does more than 'deserve forgiveness' as Johnson says of it. Mr. Power has done his utmost to annihilate every shadow of merit in the twelfth. Creech chose the thirteenth ; and performed his task like himself, unequally, but upon the whole with vigour. Johnson says, but he says it with a perhaps, ' that Creech is the only one of these trans-lators who has not lost sight of the dignity of Juvenal ; although they all, more or less, have pre-served his point.' This was a prudent 'perhaps.' John Dryden, jun. translated the Fourteenth Satire very creditably. But I fancy I see the father here again.

> Children like tender osiers take the bow,
> And as they first are fashion'd always grow.

I have given this general account of Dryden's coadjutors, because I did not think the real merit of some of them had ever been sufficiently appre-ciated. They abound in beauties, although they have many faults.

Further on, Hodgson states what he considers to have been the object of his original.

An object, which I consider a very noble one, namely, that of exposing vice in its true colours and natural deformity.

With reference to his style he quotes Johnson.

Juvenal's peculiarity is a mixture of stateliness and gaiety, of pointed sentences and declamatory grandeur.

And Gifford.

When the dignity of Juvenal is wanting, his wit will be imperfectly preserved. Wit, indeed, he possesses in an eminent degree ; but it is tinctured with his peculiarities: ' Rarò jocos, sæpius acerbos sales miscet.'[1] Dignity is the predominant quality of his mind ; he can and does relax with grace, but he never forgets himself ; he smiles indeed, but his smile is more terrible than his frown, for it is never excited but when his indignation is mingled with contempt. ' Ridet et odit.'
Mr. Gifford, in another part of his very interesting essay on the Roman satirists, observes that there is a slovenliness in some of Juvenal's verses, for which he

[1] Lipsius.

has been justly blamed, as it would have cost him so
little pains to improve them. But, generally speaking (as Mr. Gifford, by the slight exception he has
made, I suppose allows), the poetry of Juvenal has a
remarkably equable and harmonious flow. To my
ears, I confess, there is hardly among the Latin poets
one whose versification sounds more musically, or
seems to have run with less labour from the author.
Surely, then, such a writer should appear in English
with as few discontinued and broken lines as possible.
Indeed, however allowable these interruptions may
be in Latin hexameters, in English rhymes they certainly are not, when the disjointed verse recurs frequently. This may be a natural defect in the constitution of rhyme, but so it is. Pope's regular couplets,
in which one complete part, at least, of the sense of
a passage is almost always expressed, have been
censured ; but are Dryden's verses so uniformly good
when considered as couplets ? and whom besides
Dryden, as a writer of rhyme, shall we venture to
oppose to Pope ? In the general effect of harmony,
indeed, Dryden is much superior. But of that elsewhere. Goldsmith has been singularly accurate in
the terminations of his verses. They are almost
without exception perfectly symphonious. Johnson,
too, had a very correct ear. But they wrote little in

verse compared to Pope. And I question whether
the English language (with all its unpruned luxu-
riance) affords a sufficient variety of teleutic music to
prevent the occasional recurrence of a faulty rhyme
in long compositions. Spenser has done wonders in
this way as well as in all others. Milton's contempt
for rhyme is well known. When Dryden called upon
him one day to ask his permission to introduce some
of his ' Paradise Lost ' into a piece (in rhyme) which
Dryden was preparing for the theatre, ' Aye,' said
the old bard, ' you may tag my verses if you will.'

With reference to the coarseness of many passages, the translator expresses his belief that the
aim of Juvenal in writing so grossly was to lay open
the native unsightliness of vice, to remove that fascinating cloak which hides its horrors, and thereby to
render it an object too disgusting to be publicly
espoused, a guest too dangerous to be privately
admitted. The poet labours to awaken the conscience, and to put the prosperous villain to the blush
by a daringly faithful picture of the corruptions of his
country.

After a further exposition of the plan of his
poem, and a grateful recognition of the great and
unexpected patronage accorded to it, Hodgson pro-

ceeds to the Prologue, in which, after tracing the rise
and growth of satire, and drawing a pointed comparison between Juvenal and other satirists, he declares
that if, by referring the picture of Rome's depravity
to the immorality then prevalent in England, he
could ensure the reformation of one of his countrymen, the labours of his youthful muse would be
amply rewarded.

Among the contemporary critiques of the translation, the most deserving of notice is that of the
'Edinburgh Review,' which had been inaugurated a
few years before, under the auspices of Sydney
Smith, Horner, Brougham, and last, but not least,
that 'literary anthropophagus,' Jeffrey. That Hodgson's talents as a scholar and a poet were now pretty
generally appreciated is evident, not only from the
many distinguished names which are found among
the list of subscribers to his Juvenal, but also from
the fact that 'the young gentlemen' of 'the Edinburgh' condescended to consider it worthy of their
censorship, and bestowed upon it their accustomed
meed of praise and blame ; the latter, as was usual
with this periodical in the early years of its existence,
greatly exceeding the former in emphasis.   The
critique commences with a studied attempt to depreciate the genius of Juvenal himself, and, after a

sufficiently shallow criticism of his character and style, proceeds, with youthful wisdom, to lay down the law upon the subject of translations in general and translators in particular. Having expressed a preference for Johnson's imitations to any translation of Juvenal, however spirited or accurate, the review proceeds, after passing allusions to Holyday, Stapylton, and Dryden, to a comparison between the works of Gifford and Hodgson. Upon both is bestowed an almost equal share of censure and approbation.

Hodgson's extraordinary facility for versifying was, doubtless, a snare to him, and led him sometimes into unnecessary diffuseness. His easy, well-turned couplets are unfavourably criticised, and the occasional roughnesses of Mr. Gifford's translation are by the 'Edinburgh' considered to be more in the style of Juvenal, and therefore preferable to 'the unbending stateliness of Mr. Hodgson's versification.' The fact was, that the translator thought the Latin and English languages so intrinsically different in structure as to render a close imitation of style as impracticable as it was undesirable.

The translator is also found guilty on a charge of giving too frequent expression to his own originality of thought. But this fault is partly condoned. The sin that most easily besets a translator is that of

grafting his own sense on that of his original, and
the temptation is the stronger the more he is a
man of talent and imagination. Mr. Hodgson
transgresses in this respect oftener than his predecessor, but it is a liberty which, if used sparingly
and neatly, we are not much disposed to censure,
Juvenal not being, in our eyes, so perfect a poet
that nothing can be added or taken away without
injury. Instances which do no discredit to the
original occur in Sat. xiv. 187, &c.

The 'Review' continues its comparison by noticing
that the two translations are very seldom at variance
in the meaning of Juvenal, and in one or two of the
few passages when there is a difference, is 'disposed
to agree with Mr. Hodgson,' who, in the lines which
conclude the Fourth Satire, is pronounced to have
surpassed all his predecessors.

The Eleventh and Fourteenth Satires are selected
as the best in the translation, partly from their intrinsic excellence, and partly from superiority of execution. The Eighth and Tenth Satires would, the
'Review' thinks, have been better translated by Mr.
Hodgson than by the friends (Merivale and Drury) to
whom he assigned them ; and it goes on to admit
that he has great powers of easy and elegant versifi-

cation, but thinks that he has directed his intellectual labours to a department that was already overstocked, and, although denying the right to interfere with any man in the application he chooses to make of his talents, yet expresses a regret that Mr. Hodgson's had not been directed to a less hackneyed subject.

Many others might have been found more interesting to the world, and better suited to his own powers. The charm of his versification is chiefly perceptible in the descriptive parts, where the poet dwells on natural scenery, or the primitive simplicity of ancient manners.   Hence the superiority we ascribed to the Eleventh Satire, and the pleasure we derive from such lines as the following :—

> And Auster, resting in his silent cave,
> Shakes from his wing the moisture of the wave.

Now, there are several poets of antiquity that would have opened a wider field for the display of this peculiar excellence of our author; a field where he would have been less elbowed and jostled by competitors.   From the works of Statius, of whom he speaks more than once in the highest terms, and to whose merits no English translation has yet done full justice ; and of Ovid, whom he denominates 'the most beautiful of all descriptive poets,' Mr. Hodgson, we are confident, could make a selection that would delight a much more extended circle of readers than he can expect to peruse the present volume. Our confidence is grounded on some exquisite morsels he has given in the notes, as well from the poets above mentioned, as from Catullus, Claudian, Martial, &c. As we look upon these translations to be not the least valuable part of the book, we shall subjoin one or two. The beautiful address to Sleep, in the 'Sylvæ' of Statius (v. 4), which is translated at page 460, commences thus :—

> How have I wrong'd thee, Sleep, thou gentlest power
> Of heav'n ! that I alone, at night's dread hour,
> Still from thy soft embraces am repress'd,
> Nor drink oblivion on thy balmy breast?
> Now every field and every flock is thine,
> And seeming slumbers bend the mountain pine ;
> Hush'd is the tempest's howl, the torrent's roar,
> And the smooth wave lies pillow'd on the shore.

A humorous description of a parasite from Martial follows, and then that fine passage in Lucretius (v. 1217).

The Review closes with a scathing criticism of the notes, which it condemns in the most indiscriminate manner as most unnecessarily diffuse and disconnected. It must be admitted that censure on this point was to a certain degree justifiable. Hodgson's reading had been very extensive, and his memory was marvellously retentive. To this latter quality Byron bears testimony, in that passage of his journal where he refutes the assertions of his mother, Madame de Staël, and the 'Edinburgh,' that his character bore a resemblance to that of Rousseau: 'He (Rousseau) had a *bad* memory; I *had*, at least, an excellent one (ask Hodgson, the poet—a good judge, for he has an astonishing one).' This enviable faculty betrayed its possessor into excessive copiousness of illustration, but not to such an extent as to justify the unmitigated censure bestowed upon it with the utmost virulence by the 'Scotch Review.' Hodgson at twenty-seven was not a man to rest tamely under an attack which he felt to be unduly harsh. The depreciation of the great Satirist himself, and the slighting allusion to his friends and coadjutors, combined to excite his utmost indignation; and he immediately replied to the 'Review' in a spirited satire, written in the same vigorous style which, a year later, astonished the literary world in the 'English Bards and Scotch Reviewers.' His old and warm-hearted friend, William Gifford, had published an edition of Massinger, which had been 'damned with faint praise' in the same number of the 'Edinburgh' as that which contained the above-mentioned critique. Byron, whose acquaintance he had lately made, and for whose genius he had, from the first, entertained the warmest admiration, had been cruelly maltreated in his first attempt. The criticisms of several other periodicals were equally ill-judging and unjust. Hodgson felt irresistibly impelled to write, and he wrote, perhaps with more justice than discretion, as far at least as his own literary reputation was concerned.

The satirist begins by apostrophising the whole chorus of 'irresponsible, indolent reviewers' who pass hasty judgments upon youthful talent.

> But chiefly those anonymously wise,
> Who skulk in darkness from Detection's eyes,
> And high on Learning's chair affect to sit,
> The self-raised arbiters of sense and wit.

And having illustrated his statements by several recent instances which are introduced with mingled humour and severity, he proceeds to give an allegorical description of the birth, growth, and decline of the Writer's art, founded partly on the account of the Birth of Criticism in the 'Rambler,' partly on Fielding's essay on the same subject. The concluding lines are devoted to that magazine which Byron denominates My Grandmother's Review, the 'British,' and a certain book called the 'Eclectic Review,' of the existence of which the satirist informs his readers that he has heard on very credible authority, although he has never had the privilege of reading it. But as he is told that it speaks charitably of his Juvenal as a whole, and believes that its censure, if known, would rather increase than diminish his reputation, he is not disposed to resent its well-meant attempts at discriminating criticism.

CHAPTER IV.

EXTRACTS FROM REVIEWS—LETTERS FROM WIL-
LIAM GIFFORD AND DR. IRELAND—TUTORSHIP
AT KING'S.

1807-8.

THE Reviews which challenged the satire to which
reference is made in the last chapter were, as there
mentioned, the 'Edinburgh,' the 'British,' and the
'Eclectic.' There were others which spoke of the
translation in terms of the most enthusiastic praise,
tempered only by fair criticism. The 'Monthly,' while
echoing the 'Edinburgh's' censure of the diffuseness
of the notes, bore ample testimony to the vigour and
the spirit of the translation and to the beauty of its
poetry. The 'Critical' was still more eulogistic, and
this Review was distinguished for discriminating
taste. In a note in Moore's 'Life of Byron' allusion is
made to its critique on the 'Hours of Idleness,' written
in September 1807. This Review, in pronouncing
upon the young author's future career, showed itself

more prophet-like than the great oracle of the North. In noticing the elegy on Newstead Abbey, the writer says : 'We could not but hail with something of prophetic rapture the hope conveyed in the closing stanza—

> Haply thy sun, emerging, yet may shine,
> Thee to irradiate with meridian ray.

Of Hodgson's Juvenal it writes in a similar strain. It begins by expressing satisfaction at the intellectual vigour of the age which had produced Hodgson's Juvenal before Gifford's was properly digested. By way of combating the assertion that another translation was unnecessary, it mentions the circumstance that Pope's Homer appeared before Creech's was fairly finished. The ' Critical ' continues with a comparison of Hodgson and Gifford.

The lists have been cleared of all the combatants of inferior note, and are exclusively occupied by two distinguished cavaliers ; one founded from experience and reputation in a long established fame ; the other rejoicing in great though hitherto untried powers, vigorous in youth, and inflamed with the noble confidence of future glory. What must inspire every generous spectator with some degree of prejudice in favour of the young adventurer, and with the hope, at least, that he may not encounter an ignominious defeat, is the courtesy displayed by him towards his veteran adversary, whom he treats with uncommon respect and deference, and whom he loads with the most profuse and liberal praise.

After a detailed description of the style and method of the rival translators, the 'Critical' sums up its comparison by saying :—

Mr. Gifford has made a very intelligible and entertaining work; Mr. Hodgson has enriched the language of his native country by some of the noblest poetry to be found in it.

It then proceeds to particular criticisms.

In the terrible Sixth Satire Mr. Hodgson's powers appear both·original and splendid, even when contrasted with one or two most signal triumphs achieved by the genius of Dryden. Even the description of Messalina, the most finished and most spirited *morceau* that can perhaps be found in the whole translated works of that mighty master, appears to us to be rivalled by the same passage as it is represented in the volume before us. If our classical readers will compare these wonderful bursts of poetic fire, we are persuaded that they will, at least, think it doubtful to which the preference onght to be justly awarded.

A quotation from the Sixth Satire follows, and the Review remarks upon it: 'Can anything exceed the boldness, the spirit, the dramatic effect of this domestic scene?' Another quotation from Satire xii. 101. elicits a just tribute to Hodgson's talents for tender and interesting poetry, and picturesque description of natural objects.

This beautiful picture reminds one of all that is soft and fresh and brilliant in the loveliest sea-pieces of Claude, whose delicate and alluring style has been less frequently attempted by the strong hand of Juvenal than the coarser taste which suggested a copy of vulgar but striking objects to the faithful pencil of Teniers. The Third Satire proves Mr. Hodgson to possess much of the skill, humour, and correctness that distinguish the Flemish artists.[1]

The sea-piece, which suggested a comparison with Claude's painting may certainly be considered more picturesque than its original ; only those who have witnessed such a scene on the Italian coast can fully appreciate its simple grace and fidelity.

[1] *Sat.* xii. 69–82.

The ' Critical ' concludes by drawing attention to Hodgson's extraordinary talent for satire, declaring its sense of the duty of giving honour to whom honour is due, not only in justice to the author himself, but to the public, whose judgment was in danger of being misdirected by that class of critics who made it their constant practice to pass indiscriminate censure upon young aspirants to literary fame, thereby too often suppressing further endeavours. Of Mr. Hodgson the Review thought it bare justice to declare that he had displayed all the essential qualities of a poet to be found in a translation, and added a hope that there might soon be an opportunity of appreciating his claims to the higher praise of invention and original composition. Having already stated that it thought him peculiarly gifted with poetical talents, the Review is satisfied that he cannot be at a loss for proper objects on which to employ them

while our Tartuffes are daily assuming a thousand disguises, and while cold-blooded metaphysicians pretend to regulate the public taste in regard to Poetry and the Belles Lettres.

This complimentary critique was soon afterwards endorsed by Lord Byron. In one of the last stanzas of ' English Bards ' he apostrophises his Alma Mater—

whom he elsewhere terms a harsh beldam—in four forcible lines.

> Oh, dark asylum of a Vandal race !
> At once the boast of learning and disgrace !
> So lost to Phœbus that not Hodgson's verse
> Can make thee better, nor poor Hewson's worse.

And in his note on the words ' Hodgson's verse,' the noble poet writes :—

This gentleman's name requires no praise : the man who in translation displays unquestionable genius, may be well expected to excel in original composition, of which, it is to be hoped, we shall soon see a splendid specimen.

Two letters from Gifford, one written before, and the other after, the publication of the rival translations, are interesting, not only from their intrinsic excellence and from the value which must naturally belong to any composition from the pen of so eminent a man, but from the insight which they give into the literary sentiments of the great writer and critic, and the evidence which they afford of his generous sympathy with the youthful competitor for fame in the same field of literature in which he himself had so long been engaged. The first of these letters is addressed to Mr. Henry Drury at Harrow in 1806.

My dear Sir,—I ought to have written long since, but
I may say to you in confidence what the beggar
said to Louis XIV. : 'O sir, if you did but know
how idle I am, you would pity me!'

I am delighted with your good opinion of
Massinger.[1] I take refuge in our old plays, from
the execrable trash of the present stage ; and
should, in my plodding way, have no objection to
revise the twin-writers of whom you speak, who
abound in beauties of every description : but I am
not rich enough to do it at my own expense, and
the booksellers engage with reluctance in whatever
does not promise an immediate sale. Peter
Whalley, who edited Ben Jonson, amassed, before
his last illness, a world of lumber preparatory to a
second edition. In his hands it must have grown
to fourteen volumes at least, for he had unfortunately discovered with what ease a book might be
swelled out by parallel passages. This has been
put into my hands. His collections, I find, have
been plundered by Steevens and Malone, who
wisely kept their secret—to me they are useless :
yet I am not certain, if my sight does not totally
fail me, but that I may be tempted to reprint the
original with the additions of scenery, &c., some-

____

[1] Gifford was then engaged in editing the dramas of Massinger.

what in the manner of Massinger, to facilitate the understanding of him, which now requires more attention than the general reader can or will bestow.

Juvenal drags heavily. At one time, all Bulwer's devils, arrant, passant, couchant, and rampant, are at my heels, roaring for copy ; at another I cannot get sight of them ; and if I make inquiries —why they are gone for twelve days to get drunk with the blameless Ethiopians. So we proceed. I take it for granted that Mr. Hodgson is not more fortunate. In this edition, I have added a little, and but a little, to the notes, and attempted here and there to squeeze the text a little together. I have no idea of improving it, unless, as Sir J. Cutler's maid—absit invidia—improved his stockings. I want a poetical friend, for the gods have not made the Dr.[1] poetical, and most of my other acquaintance are over ears in politicks (*sic*).

I have scarcely been out of doors since I wrote last. You would therefore have found me in my elbow chair, and I should have been truly proud and happy to have seen you. I am now meditating a south sea voyage to Newmarket for a fortnight or three weeks, as I have some reliance on a change

[1] Dean Ireland.

of air. 'Pray make me happy,' as Scindiah says, 'by your letters.'

Ever, my dear Sir, most sincerely yours,

WM. GIFFORD.

The second letter, addressed to Hodgson himself, gives pleasing proof of the generosity and true nobility of mind of one of nature's gentlemen.

James Street : Monday Night.

Though the Dr. and I had respectively ordered Juvenal to be sent to us the moment it appeared, yet your active kindness has, with me, anticipated the plodding industry of the bookseller. I accept your present with the sincerest pleasure and shall ever regard it among my choicest possessions.

I fell on it immediately, and, without removing my eye for an instant from the page, read, shall I say devoured? the six first satires—more I could not do—nor do I expect to be able to distinguish an 'a' from a 'b' for the next twenty-four hours.

In simplicity and truth I am delighted with you ; for the haste and imperfection of which you speak, I see nothing but freedom, spirit, and vigour : your anxiety I place to the score of modesty ; it is surely not necessary, but I do not condemn it. Would you could impart a little of it, where it is really needed! 'But fools rush in,' you know. Expect to hear nothing of the Introduction and Notes, for I have not read a syllable of them yet.

I am amazed at the facility (to say nothing of the elegance) with which you compose ; though Ireland, who regards you with great affection, had, in some measure, prepared me for it. Your morning's amusement would occupy me seriously for a week—and Jove only knows what it would be after all. And have you the conscience, with all this ease and spirit and learning and extensive reading, to call upon me to improve your trial? pro pudor!

No, no ; you must look upon me as an old post-horse : what with switching and spurring I might perhaps perform a short stage ; but should be mighty stiff after it, and not in a travelling condition for some time. Do you recollect that I once said 'mox in reluct :' &c. I had then no bad idea, and, as I thought, not unproductive of useful fun. It was a work on the plan of 'Le chef-d'œuvre d'un Inconnu,' that genuine piece of French humour. I had written the life of my 'Hero,' containing, with great pomposity, not one accident that does not happen to every clown every day of his life ; I had also composed a poem—oh such a poem! I do not think 'Jack Horner' came within a league of it ; and amassed a vast quantity of illustrations 'after the manner' of all sorts of people, to render every clear point incomprehensible ; and many other pretty things. When I had done all this, 'an exposition of idleness,' as Bottom says—not your friend Flatbottom Urgius whose *various reading* is very good—but an 'exposition of idleness' came upon me, and before I recovered my activity, a storm or robbery, call it which you will, 'shook down my mellow hangings.' To secure my precious arcana I wisely put them within an old chessboard, taking care to secure them with a string that, like Styx, went nine times round it. 'If you have tears, prepare to shed them now.' In changing houses, this casket, to which that of Alexander was but a tin canister, was conveyed out of the cart that bore the curta supellex. I consoled myself in my distress by reflecting on the disappointment of the miserable thief of a rascal when he opened his *purchase.* But why do I tell you this cock and bull story? Firstly, that you may take up my design—you have fifty times more talents for it than I had in my best days ; and surely the harvest is richer than ever—et quando uberior ?—O what giggling might you have at the Germans! to say nothing of the home produce.

My valued friends in Gower Street told me of your removal to Cambridge : on this I felicitate you, and, let me add, the world, most sincerely ; for you will certainly have more time at command. I thank you for your congratulations ; presuming that you allude to the lottery. Nothing is yet settled, but I believe some good is *en train*. Down on your knees and be thankful that you see land at last. The watchman is now bellowing just two o'clock. With the sincerest esteem,

I remain your obliged and faithful friend,

WM. GIFFORD.

The removal to Cambridge, to which allusion is made in this letter, refers to Hodgson's appointment to a Resident Tutorship at King's College of which he had already for five years been a fellow. Humphrey Sumner, the then Provost, had asked him to lecture upon Locke and Pearson. Hodgson replied in the following letter, in which he sketches in outline some of the views with which he entered upon his new sphere of work.

Eton : October 1, 1807.

Dear Sir,—I am greatly obliged by your keeping the tutorship open for me so long ; and lament the

necessity of my absence from Cambridge till
Christmas.

Concerning the subject of my lectures I am
very glad to have the opportunity of some communication with you. The books you mention
(Locke and Pearson) are as yet by no means
among my intimate acquaintance; but I will take
the liberty of offering my general ideas of their
character to your consideration. Upon Butler, I
believe, we are agreed, that his 'Analogy' is too
profound a work for any but the severest student
to comprehend. At the lectures by Mr. Lloyd
which I attended at Cambridge, I gathered that
there was much in Locke controverted by subsequent reasoners ; but I did not perceive that anything had been added to the explanation and argument of Pearson for a succession of years. Of the
effect which Mr. Lloyd's lectures had upon his
hearers, as all were at the same college with myself,
I can form some opinion. It is an assured truth
that not one pupil out of a dozen gained anything
from the Locke lecture when I was at college. But
Mr. Lloyd has made Locke the study of his life.
If then, with his excellent understanding and long
application, he could not render the lecture interesting or useful, how is another person to do it ? It is

my belief that in the ' Essay on the Human Understanding' Mr. Locke is often bewildered in the
subtlety of his own reasoning. Nothing is so dark
as metaphysical speculation, and nothing, therefore,
requires so plain a light to be thrown upon it.
That Mr. Locke's manner is popular, or likely to
catch the attention of young men, I cannot allow.
It is very different with Pearson. His reasoning is
clear, intelligible, and convincing. I do not, then,
despair of being able ' to tell the tale as 'tis told
me,' which is the chief thing required in a lecture extracted from Pearson ; but I do despair of
forcibly recommending the fine-spun lucubrations
of Mr. Locke to the attention of my pupils.

I have written this letter very hastily, in the
midst of uncongenial employment, and of hard addi-
tional labour at my publication. You will therefore,
I trust, excuse any misstatement of opinion expressed upon the moment, though not formed without previous consideration. The fact is, that ever
since your kind promise of appointing me to the
tutorship, I have found my thoughts naturally
engaged in my few leisure hours with the business
of my future work. And I will request your
permission to enter a little further into the result of
my reflections. Young men are but three years at

King's, and any very accurate knowledge of a philosophical work cannot be communicated to them by an hour's explanation every day in the half terms. That the generality of young men will take much trouble to prepare themselves for lectures is not to be expected. A few will really examine their work beforehand; a few more will just run it over; but the greater part will not look at it till the moment. Still they may learn something, they may all learn something, if the subject is interesting, and if their instructor adapts his manner to their prejudices and their turn of thought. But I contend that a metaphysical subject is not generally interesting, although a religious subject is more so than any other; and, as to manner, the young are all impatient of delay. If a lecturer is slow, they conceive that he is stupid, and then the business is done. Now, I question whether any but the most superficial knowledge of Locke could be imparted without a very cautious slowness of interpretation. . . .

Since I left college my reading has been very miscellaneous. It has chiefly been devoted to Greek and Latin authors, but has diverged a good deal into French and English literature. Lectures upon the Belles Lettres, in short, have been my principal study. I do not pretend to any *deep* knowledge here; neither my age nor my other engagements can have allowed much proficiency. But, having read Rollin and Blair when a boy, a third set of lectures upon the same subject was put into my hands some years since by a lecturer of the name of Barron. He has not, I think, supplied many of the deficiencies of his predecessors, although in his essay on Logic he has, I think, done more than they had attempted. What I fancied worth remembering in my own reading I always noted down, and when I was requested, not long since, to give a collected opinion of these writers, I interwove my own observations with extracts and opinions from their works. This employment, and the translation of Juvenal, have, with other occasional exertions of the same kind, filled my time since I left college ; and I mention these circumstances to introduce a proposal which, had I not waited for some previous intimation from you upon the subject, I should have submitted to your consideration a month ago. Suppose a lecture upon Belles Lettres —a general account of the sages, historians, orators, and poets of Greece and Rome. For instance, Demosthenes ; the character of his age, the state of Greece, and of Athens particularly, when he flourished ; the history and effect of his orations ; a comparison between his style and that of other orators. Or, to make the lecture more general, it might embrace a connected account of all the principal Greek and Roman writers, the examination of their style, with extracts from their works ; and a general comparison of ancient and modern literature might be made both pleasant and useful. Quinctilian, Longinus, Diogenes Laertius, Macrobius, would open their stores to me, nor have I mentioned the treasure of treasures, Aristotle. Surely one could blend a spell from them all enough to attract the Old Court.

I request your indulgence for this imperfect exposition of a plan of lectures; but, as I look forward to Cambridge as my residence for many years, and enter upon that residence under your auspices (quod spiro et placeo, si placeo, tuum est), I think it right to make you as much acquainted as I am with my views and inclinations before entering upon my employment.

Whether so extraordinary a development of the customary curriculum at King's was allowed is doubtful. But there can be no doubt that, in Hodgson's hands, it would have been universally admitted to be a most refreshing novelty. All changes in those days were looked upon with suspicion. The provost, Humphrey Sumner, was a person of staid conservative principles. His naturally ponderous manner and disposition were still further retarded by deafness; an infirmity of which it is sad to reflect that Ben Drury, the Eton master, should ever have taken advantage, to the infinite amusement of those present, by making most uncomplimentary observations to him in the manner of a person conversing upon some ordinary topic—observations which were invariably received with the blandest courtesy.

Notwithstanding Hodgson's diffidence in the matter of the Locke lecture, the Provost persisted in his request, and Hodgson, accordingly, at once applied himself to the study of metaphysics. Some of his written lectures which remain prove him to have thoroughly mastered his subject, and to have presented it to his pupils in so pleasant and attractive a form as must have met with ample appreciation from undergraduate understandings. But, not content with these masterly expositions, his poetical mind, as usual, had recourse to verses for a fuller expression of those deep imaginings which his metaphysical research had naturally suggested to it, and in the 'Ballad on Metaphysics,' written at this time, he gives an epitome of the whole subject, inclusive of the systems of Aristotle, Descartes, Locke, and Reid; contriving to invest even abstract reasoning with poetical harmony, and concluding with some lines of great power and beauty on the legitimate end and consummation of all human studies—the adoration of the Deity.

As in a measure appropriate to the subject of metaphysics, some letters by the Rev. John Ireland, then prebendary, afterwards the distinguished Dean of Westminster, may here be given. His early acquaintance with Hodgson has already been noticed, and the high opinion which he had formed of his character and abilities is plainly proved by the tone of these letters.

In a note to the Second Satire of Juvenal Hodgson had written with reference to the accusations sometimes brought against his original that he ridiculed the idea of a future state.

Did not Socrates in his dying hours use the common language of his countrymen with regard to the gods, and yet we cannot suppose him to have intended more than an example of conformity to established usage when he enjoined the sacrifice of a cock to Esculapius; although we know he believed in *an all-wise and all-powerful Creator and Supporter of the Universe.*

Hodgson's naturally reverent mind and early religious training here, no doubt, betrayed him into the use of an expression similar to those commonly current among Churchmen. He probably did not mean to say more than that Socrates believed in the Supreme Governor of the universe, which in its state of order owed Him alone its existence; and did not intend to enter at all into the question of ancient beliefs in pre-existent matter. With this point of view, as far as it goes, the Scriptural doctrine is not materially at variance, when it distinctly asserts that the Creator brought Cosmos out of Chaos.

But the erudite Dr. Ireland, the author of 'Five Discourses containing certain Arguments for and against the Reception of Christianity by the ancient Jews and Greeks,' of 'Paganism and Christianity compared,' and many other profound theological dissertations, was not likely to rest satisfied with any mode of expression in the annotation of a classical work which could possibly admit of misinterpretation on such a point. He accordingly wrote in the following strain, which if hypercritical must be considered to have been not the less complimentary to a man who was twenty years younger than himself :—

Croydon : January 11, 1808.

Dear Sir,—I have begun to read your Juvenal; and you will judge from what I am about to say, how strong is my remembrance of the esteem which I felt for you several years ago, when my intercourse with you and your family was nearer than it is at present.

In one of the notes to the Second Satire, it is said, in vindication of the character of Socrates, that he believed in an all-powerful Creator of the universe. I am persuaded, from the general complexion of the assertion, that you cannot have made a *regular* inquiry into this part of the Pagan theology. I am persuaded, too, that, if you had, your mind would have arrived at the same conviction which I feel. It has happened that, for a theological purpose, I have looked with some attention into this point ; and of nothing am I more firmly convinced, than that in no Pagan school was ever taught the doctrine of a proper creation. It happens, too, that, at this very time, I am engaged in impressing this religious caution upon the King's scholars at Westminster, to whom I read term lectures. It is highly probable that your translation may fall into the hands of such youths; and I should be extremely unwilling to hear that their belief in an essential and peculiar doctrine of Revelation was likely to be unsettled by any contrary observation of yours. If when you did me the honour of calling here, I had been aware of this circumstance I should have taken the liberty of a friend, and requested that you would have placed the passage in question at my disposal. However, all this depends on the confidence which you might have in my research or my judgment. The best thing to be done is to look into this important point yourself before another edition of your book is called for. If I should be so fortunate as to meet with you before that time comes, perhaps I might be able to prove my assertion even by conversation.

I have troubled you with a long letter; but I believe that I know your heart, and that you will take what I have said as a private mark of friendship.

I beg you to believe me, dear Sir,
Yours very truly,
J. IRELAND.

No. 1 Fludyer Street : March 28, 1808.

Dear Sir,—Your letter has found me here, being engaged in the duties of my residence, and removed from the books which would have afforded me the evidence proper for the point between us. As it is, I have only the opportunity of saying that in the conclusion of your letter you have seized the word, under which lay the whole force of my observation. I had talked to you of the ignorance of the Pagan schools in the doctrine of a proper creation. By this I meant, that in all the ancient cosmology which has descended to us, the only doctrine taught is that of the form impressed upon bodies, or the extraction of bodies from pre-existing matter; and that the primary matter, or ὕλη, is always supposed beforehand. The more you examine the ancient evidence with this view, the more persuaded you will be that all these passages, in which there is an appearance of creation, are to be popularly interpreted, and that as the early Church teaches us through Eusebius, 'It was peculiar to the Hebrew doctrines to consider the God over all, the one maker of all things, and of the substance which underlies bodies, which the Greeks denominate matter.' I cannot refer to the place, for I have not my Eusebius with me, but am sure of the passage. I know that several of the fathers talked of a creation, as really inculcated by the Pagan writers; but I know that this untenable notion was advanced by them with no other view than to win the later Greeks to the Gospel through an approximation of the former Grecian writings to the Scriptures. This was one of those injudicious accommodations of which the fathers were often guilty, upon motives of mere Christian zeal. And you may be persuaded of the futility of this doctrine, when you consider that the fathers have adduced numbers of their proofs from the poets and play-writers—Sophocles, Menander, Philemon, &c. In short, I will only beg you to read a short, but perfectly convincing treatise on this subject. I mean that of Mosheim, 'De Creatione Mundi ex nihilo ; ' you will find it among his 'opuscula,' or in his edition of Cudworth's 'Intellectual System,' which indeed ought never to be read without it.

And now I must bid you farewell, for a thousand things press upon me. I have given your kind remembrance to Gifford, who is but just recovered from a fever which gave me, for a day or two, some uneasiness about him.

Hodgson's Juvenal was dedicated to his father's old friend and patron Lord Liverpool, whose gratifying acknowledgment of the dedication may fitly conclude the present chapter.

Hertford Street: Dec. 23, 1807

Dear Sir,—I received the evening before last the present you sent me of your translation of Juvenal. I have hitherto had time only to peruse the Preface: it is replete with good erudition, and with many sagacious remarks. I have no doubt that this work will do you great credit, and that I shall also derive some credit from your having done me the honour of dedicating it to me.

I am, with great truth,

Your faithful, humble servant,

LIVERPOOL.

F. Hodgson, Esq.

CHAPTER V.

COMMENCEMENT OF FRIENDSHIP WITH LONSDALE
AND LORD BYRON—NOTES OF THE LATTER ON
POPE—HIS RELIGIOUS IMPRESSIONS—LETTERS
FROM BYRON AND GIFFORD—INSTITUTION OF
THE 'QUARTERLY'—PUBLIC ORATORSHIP—
POLITICAL ALLUSIONS—LINES TO LONSDALE.

1808–9.

EARLY in 1808 Hodgson commenced his residence at
Cambridge as a fellow and tutor of King's College.
This residence continued until his marriage in 1814,
and, during this period, besides his duties and studies
at the university itself, he went each year to Rugby
as classical examiner, passed many of his vacations in
London, and was continually engaged in literary pursuits ; constantly contributing to the 'Critical' and
'Monthly' Reviews, of which last periodical he was for
some time an editor, and publishing several volumes
of poetry.

It was at this time that two young men of remarkable talent were added to the number of his
intimate friends, to each of whom Hodgson felt himself to be placed more or less in the position of
Mentor. One of them was John Lonsdale, afterwards
a rival candidate for the provostship of Eton, and
Bishop of Lichfield. The other was that brilliant,
wayward young poet who was destined to add
undying lustre to the literature of his country, and to
achieve for himself an endless fame.

The intimacy with Lord Byron, now firmly
cemented, had doubtless been formed previously
during Hodgson's visits to London and Cambridge
and to the Drurys at Harrow. The tone of the first
remaining letters denotes a degree of friendship which
must evidently have existed for some time before
they were written. But it is equally evident that the
two could not have been much thrown together without becoming intimate. There were many points of
resemblance in their characters, and enough of difference to produce harmony. An early familiarity with
and earnest admiration for the inspired writings of
the Bible, and especially of the Psalms, a love of history, of philosophy and, above all, of poetry, were
common to both, and were enough in themselves to
provide endless subjects of mutual interest for discus-

sion. Add to this that both were high-spirited and warm-hearted, genial and animated in society, but equally subject to periods of melancholy and depression when alone, and it is easy to understand the cordial affection and regard which they mutually entertained for one another throughout the period of their friendship; a friendship which continued unimpaired until Byron's final departure from England caused the partial severance of every social tie. Even then they occasionally corresponded, and there was no diminution in their mutual feelings of regard up to the time of the premature death in 1824.

In March 1808 Byron came to Cambridge for the purpose of availing himself of his privilege as a nobleman and taking his M.A. degree, although he had only matriculated in 1805. From this time, until early in 1816, the friends constantly met, and, when absent, as constantly corresponded. On this occasion of meeting there was one especial circumstance which doubtless greatly contributed to mutual sympathy. Both had been recently subjected to the fiery ordeal of criticism in the 'Edinburgh Review.' Hodgson, as we have seen, had already answered his critics in a satire of no ordinary spirit and power. Byron's still more caustic and comprehensive reply was now in process of concoction. Much must have passed between them upon this subject, and manifold must have been the notes which were compared, many and various the living poets whose relative merits and demerits must have been discussed.

Their early tastes in poetry were, moreover, much alike. Both were zealous disciples of Dryden, both entertained the deepest reverence for the genius of Pope. Hodgson's allegiance to the muse of Dryden was founded upon admiration for the intensity of its power and vigour, while Byron's veneration for Pope's style amounted almost to idolatry, and he strove to emulate with slavish exactness that correctness of form which distinguished the 'Bard of the Thames.' But in spite of what he conceived to be his better judgment, his native force and genius quickly carried him beyond the limits thus assigned, and, although in theory he ever remained loyal to his early faith, in practice he was more revolutionary than most of his predecessors and contemporaries, and soon created a style which was essentially his own.

Some fragmentary opinions which Byron jotted down as they occurred to him at this time, although wholly without method or connection, may be found interesting if inserted here.

In Ruffhead's 'Life of Pope,' a book bearing the autograph inscription 'Byron—Cambridge, A.D., 1808,' which afterwards passed into Hodgson's possession, there are a few short pointed notes in Byron's handwriting, the first of which, written hastily on a fly-leaf at the beginning, are evidently intended as criticisms, not less general than concise, of Pope's style and character as a poet. They are as follows :—

Of Pope's pithy conciseness of style Swift—no diffuse writer himself—has so emphatically said—

> For Pope can in one couplet fix
> More sense than I can do in six.

Imitators of Horace and Juvenal were Boileau and Pope—of one as well as of the other of whom it may be said—

> Même en imitant toujours original.

At the commencement of the biography Pope's personal characteristics are summarily disposed of by a short quotation scrawled in the margin.

Mr. Rawlinson of Sarsden House was a friend and correspondent of Pope. Mr. R. said that Pope was a troublesome friend and an implacable enemy— who sometimes forgot favours, but never forgave injuries.

Again, as a foot-note to the preface, and *à propos*

of nothing in the text of the biography, Byron writes :—

Pope's Nymph of the Grot bears so striking a resemblance to the delicacy of thought expressed in the following lines that one is almost tempted to suspect him of plagiarism.

AD IMAGINEM NYMPHÆ DORMIENTIS.

Hujus nympha loci, sacri custodia fontis,
 Dormio—dum blandæ sentio murmur aquæ ;
Parce meum, quisquis tangis cava marmora, Somnum
 Rumpere, sive bibas sive lavêre, tace.

This was formerly in the Villa Julia at Rome, and is copied from the 'Variorum in Europâ itinerum deliciæ,' edit. secund., 1599, by Nathan Chytiæus ; the book is very scarce.

On Mr. Ruffhead's favourable criticisms of the 'Rape of the Lock' Byron succinctly remarks :—

In the 'Rape of the Lock' Pope was indebted for his idea of the machinery to the 'Comte de Gabalis' of the Abbé Villars, and for the account of their various employments to Shakspeare's 'Tempest,' and 'Midsummer Night's Dream.' The description of the 'game of ombre' is imitated from the 'Scacchia' of Victor. In other parts of the poem he has introduced frequent parodies of Homer, Virgil, and Milton. He has also judiciously employed the celebrated fiction of Ariosto—that all things lost on earth are treasured in the moon. In this receptacle of the lunar sphere, says Ariosto, are to be found

Le lachrime, e i sospiri de gli amanti, &c. &c.

Orlando Furioso, canto 34.

Further on in the biography Mr. Ruffhead writes :—

Our author having, by his translation of Homer and other works, placed himself in circumstances of affluence, he was now at liberty to follow the true bent of his genius. The independence of his fortune did not make him negligent of his fame, nor unmindful in the duty which he owed to society, in the application of those talents which nature had so bountifully bestowed upon him. His natural benevolence suggested to him that he could not better serve the interest of society, than, as himself expresses it, by writing a book to bring mankind to look upon this life with comfort and pleasure, and put morality in good humour.

In this passage Byron underlines the word *mankind*, and writes in the margin, 'A malignant race with Christianity in their mouths and Molochism in their hearts.'   An early evidence this of that gloomy misanthropy into which the 'poet of pain,' as he has been called, loved to chafe his troubled spirit, but which was as alien from the daily practice of his life as it was from his true nature.

But there was another subject of discussion which was still more interesting to the friends, and which excited greater differences of opinion.   Byron's acquaintance with Charles Skinner Matthews, a young man of consummate ability and of brilliant promise, whose sentiments on religious subjects were avowedly sceptical, had, in the previous year, ripened into intimacy, and had, doubtless, assisted considerably in confirming those doubts and difficulties respecting revealed religion which Byron entertained, and of which the seeds had been sown in early boyhood by the rigid doctrines of Calvinism.   These doctrines had been instilled into his infant mind with uncompromising firmness, and as soon as his reasoning powers had full scope for their future development they revolted from the tyranny under which they had previously been held in check, and rejected as illogical so narrow-minded and bigoted a system.   That the reaction had set in some years before is proved by the religious poems contained in the boyish

publication entitled ‘ Hours of Idleness.’   In the
‘ Prayer of Nature,’ which breathes throughout a spirit
of deep devotion to the Deity, all systems are equally
repudiated.   Temples cannot confine the Omnipotent
within their precincts, therefore they demand no
especial reverence ; to no one sect or religious body
are His mercies and His promises confined ; it is
therefore immaterial to which men belong.   From
such a vague denial of the responsibilities of revealed
religion, the step to an actual rejection of such religion was not a long one.   And in the case of Byron
the progress in the direction of absolute disbelief was
considerably accelerated by the fascinating friendship
of that clever and witty companion to whom we have
referred, and who made no secret of his profession of
atheism.

Hodgson, as we have seen, had recently renewed
his interest in the study of metaphysics ; but so sound
had been the religious training of his youth, so deep
and sincere was his natural piety, that he was neither
at this time nor at any other period of his life in any
danger of making shipwreck of the faith.   Not that
his eyes were ever closed to the manifold difficulties
which beset the most perfect creed of an imperfect
race.   But being fully persuaded in his own mind of
the validity of the main and vital truths of revealed

religion, no vain imaginings, no shallow scepticisms or fascinating fallacies of knowledge, falsely so called, could shake his firm and unwavering faith in the authenticity of Bible doctrine; and with all the earnestness of long-cherished conviction he strove to bring back his young companion's wandering footsteps into the paths of everlasting peace.

How different might have been the short sad story of Byron's life if only the wise and affectionate counsel of his friend had received the attention and consideration which it deserved! That it had more weight than its recipient cared to admit is proved by the tone of some letters on religion which were written in 1811 in answer to Hodgson's arguments in conversation and correspondence. Underneath the reckless statements which these letters contain there runs a current of deep religious conviction, and belief in the goodness and mercy of God, which at several subsequent periods came to the surface in acts of really Christian forbearance and charity, and which, towards the end of his life, found a vent in constant perusal of the Scriptures and, at the last, in submissive acquiescence in the Divine Will.

That Byron was his own worst enemy has often been noticed by his biographers. His extraordinary love of a bad reputation, of exhibiting himself in the most unfavourable aspect, amounted almost to insanity, and was in nothing more conspicuous than in his determination to represent his religious opinions as far more sceptical than they really were. Many of his friends, and in particular Hodgson and Scrope Berdmore Davies, a fellow of King's at this time and mutual friend of Byron and Hodgson, used constantly to make fun of this idiosyncrasy. Byron, when absorbed in thought and indulging in reckless speculations, used often, as he expressed it, to suffer from 'a confusion of ideas,' and would sometimes exclaim in his most melodramatic manner, 'I shall go mad.' Scrope Davies, a true friend, and a charming vivacious companion, who had a quaint dry manner of speaking and an irresistible stammer, used quietly to remark in answer, 'Much more like silliness than madness.'

In the autumn of 1808, Byron having partially repaired Newstead, was anxious to assemble his friends around him with as little delay as possible. With this intent he wrote many pressing invitations to Hodgson, which do not appear to have been accepted until some months later. In the meantime several letters passed between them, the first which remains from Byron being dated Newstead Abbey, Nov. 3, 1808.

My dear Hodgson,—I expected to have heard ere this the event of your interview with the mysterious Mr. Hayne, my volunteer correspondent ; however, as I had no business to trouble you with the adjustment of my concerns with that illustrious stranger, I have no right to complain of your silence. Hobhouse and your humble are still here. Hobhouse hunts, &c., and I do nothing. We dined the other day with a neighbouring esquire (not Collet of Staines), and regretted your absence, as the banquet of Staines was scarcely to be compared to our last 'feast of Reason.' You know laughing is the sign of a rational animal, so says Dr. Smollett ; I think so too, but unluckily my spirits don't always keep pace with my opinions. I had not so much scope for risibility the other day as I could have wished, for I was seated near a woman, to whom, when a boy, I was as much attached as boys generally are, and more than a man should be. I knew this before I went, and was determined to be valiant, and converse with *sang froid*, but, instead, I forgot my valour and my nonchalance, and never opened my lips even to laugh, far less to speak, and the lady was almost as absurd as myself, which made both the objects of more observation than if we had conducted ourselves with easy indifference.   You will think all this great nonsense; if you had seen it you would have thought it still more ridiculous.

I have tried for Gifford's Epistle to Pindar, and the bookseller says the copies were cut up for *waste paper*: if you can procure me a copy I shall be much obliged.   Adieu!

Believe me yours ever sincerely,

BYRON.

It was about the middle of this month that the faithful favourite 'Boatswain' died, a dog whose name is almost as famous as his master's.   This sad event was at once announced to Hodgson in a characteristically tragic letter, of which Moore quotes the most important sentence.

Boatswain is dead! he expired in a state of madness on the 18th, after suffering much, yet retaining all the gentleness of his nature to the last, never attempting to do the least injury to anyone near him.   I have now lost everything except old Murray.

The next letter begins in the same melancholy strain.

Newstead Abbey, Notts : Nov. 27, 1808.

My dear Sir,—Boatswain is to be buried in a vault waiting for myself. I have also written an epitaph, which I would send, were it not for two reasons : one is, that it is too long for a letter ; and the other, that I hope you will some day read it on the spot where it will be engraved.

You discomfit me with the intelligence of the real orthodoxy of the 'Arch-fiend's' name, but alas! it must stand with me at present ; if ever I have an opportunity of correcting, I shall liken him to Geoffrey of Monmouth, a noted liar in his way, and perhaps a more correct prototype than the Carnifex of James II.

I do not think the composition of your poem 'a sufficing reason' for not keeping your promise of a Christmas visit. Why not come? I will never disturb you in your moments of inspiration ; and if you wish to collect any materials for the *scenery*, Hardwicke (where Mary was confined for several years) is not eight miles distant, and, independent of the interest you must take in it as her vindicator,[1] is a most beautiful and venerable object of curiosity. I shall take it very ill if you do not come ;

---

[1] Hodgson was writing a poem at this time on Mary Queen of Scots.

my mansion is improving in comfort, and, when you require solitude, I shall have an apartment devoted to the purpose of receiving your poetical reveries.

I have heard from our Drury; he says little of the Row, which I regret: indeed I would have sacrificed much to have contributed in any way (as a school-boy) to its consummation; but Butler survives, and thirteen boys have been expelled in vain. Davies is not here, but Hobhouse hunts as usual, and your humble servant 'drags at each remove a lengthened chain.' I have heard from his Grace of Portland on the subject of my expedition: he talks of diffi-culties; by the gods! if he throws any in my way I will next session ring such a peal in his ears,

> That he shall wish the fiery Dane
> Had rather been his guest again.

You do not tell me if Gifford is really my com-mentator: it is too good to be true, for I know nothing would gratify my vanity so much as the reality; even the idea is too precious to part with.

I still expect you here; let me have no more excuses. Hobhouse desires his best remembrance. We are now lingering over our evening potations.

I have extended my letter further than I ought, and beg you will excuse it ; on the opposite page I send you some stanzas I wrote off on being questioned by a former flame as to my motives for quitting this country. You are the first reader. Hobhouse hates everything of the kind, therefore I do not show them to him. Adieu !

Believe me yours very sincerely,

BYRON.

Moore gives extracts from other letters written about the same time as the preceding. In one of his answers Hodgson had remarked, jestingly, that some of the verses in 'Hours of Idleness' were calculated to make schoolboys rebellious. This suggested a comparison with Tyrtæus, and an allusion to that lameness of which the sensitive poet so often spoke with a sort of good-humoured sarcasm.

If my songs have produced the glorious effects you mention, I shall be a complete Tyrtæus ; though I am sorry to say that I resemble that interesting harper more in his person than in his poesy.

Hodgson remembered an occasion, also mentioned by Moore, when, in a large and mixed company, a vulgar person asked Byron aloud, ' Pray, my Lord, how is that foot of yours?' 'Thank you, Sir,' answered Lord Byron, with the utmost mildness, 'much the same as usual.'

The next letter is written in so light and playful a strain, and is such a remarkable contrast to the melancholy style of those which precede it, that the fragmentary form in which it appears in Moore's Life can only be accounted for by supposing that some of its allusions were considered likely to wound living sensibilities.   However this may have been, there can be no possible reason for suppressing any of it, after the lapse of nearly seventy years.

Newstead Abbey, Notts: Dec. 17, 1808.

My dear Hodgson,—I have just received your letter, and one from B. Drury, which I would send, were it not too bulky to despatch within a sheet of paper ; but I must impart the contents and consign the answer to your care.   In the first place, I cannot address the answer to him, because the epistle is without date or direction ; and in the next, the contents are so singular that I can scarce believe my optics, 'which are made the fools of the other senses, or else worth all the rest.'

A few weeks ago, I wrote to our friend Harry Drury of facetious memory, to request he would prevail on his brother at Eton to receive the son of a citizen of London well known unto me as a pupil; the family having been particularly polite during the short time I was with them, induced me to this application. 'Now mark what follows,' as somebody or Southey sublimely saith : on this day, the 17th December, arrives an epistle signed B. Drury, containing, not the smallest reference to tuition or *in*tuition, but a *petition* for *Robert Gregson*, of pugilistic notoriety, now in bondage for certain paltry pounds sterling, and liable to take up his everlasting abode in Banco Regis. Had this letter been from any of my *lay* acquaintance, or, in short, from any person but the gentleman whose signature it bears, I should have marvelled not. If Drury is serious I congratulate pugilism on the acquisition of such a patron, and shall be happy to advance any sum necessary for the liberation of the captive Gregson; but I certainly hope to be certified from you or some reputable housekeeper of the fact, before I write to Drury on the subject. When I say the *fact* I mean of the *letter* being written by *Drury*, not having any doubt as to the authenticity of the statement. The letter is now before me, and I keep it for your perusal. When I hear from you I shall address my answer to him, under *your* *care*; for as it is now the vacation at Eton, and the letter is without *time* or *place*, I cannot venture to consign my sentiments on so *momentous* a *concern* to chance.

To you, my dear Hodgson, I have not much to say. If you can make it convenient or pleasant to trust yourself here, be assured it will be both to me.

Before this year (1808) came to an end Hodgson went to Newstead ; but there is no record of this first visit, except a copy, which he took at the time when they were composed, of the celebrated lines inscribed by Byron on the cup formed from a skull, together with a rough sketch of the cup itself.

Early in the following year we find Hodgson in correspondence with Gifford on literary subjects, and actively engaged in writing for Reviews. On April 25, 1809, Gifford writes from James Street :—

My dear Sir,—Business and illness have conspired to prevent me from noticing your obliging note before. I have just been with Murray, and discovered that your conjecture is well founded. I therefore, with great pleasure, entrust the 'Four Slaves'[1] to your

---

[1] The 'Four Slaves of Cythera,' by the Rev. Robert Bland, editor of the celebrated 'Anthology,' and author of 'Edwy and Elgiva,' and other poems.

care. . . . I have read the poem with great satisfaction. Is the plan of it original, or formed on
some legend? It is wild enough for an Arabian
tale, but probability is not of much moment.
There are many beautiful flights of genuine poetry
of the good old English stamp. The light parts
are very pleasant, but a passage here and there is
too familiar. There are, besides, a few ungram-
matical terms; things not improper to be noticed,
especially when the general merit is so great. I
hope that Mr. Bland is by this time recovered.
I puzzled him sorely the other day by sending him
a letter destined for a grave divine; but it may be
some consolation to him to know that I puzzled
the said divine still more.

The translation of Hesiod, if you have leisure
and inclination, is very much at your service. I
have just looked into it. The poetry, I suppose,
is well enough for the subject, which is neither
very amusing nor very interesting. The notes are
stuffed out with corrections of Cooke; about as
wise a process, as if we had employed ourselves in
the correction of Rhodes. There is also a vast
deal taken from Jacob Bryant's ' Mythology,' which,
I thought, no one at present ever looked at without

a smile. The Doctor[1] is much pleased with your approbation of his book ; it cost him much pains— whether they might have been better bestowed, this deponent sayeth not ; but he has pleased the Westminsters. Autant de gagné!

Ever, my dear Sir,

Most sincerely yours,

WM. GIFFORD.

P.S. You are right. I have no northern coadjutor but Scott ;[2] at least, at present.

From the same to the same.

James Street, Buckingham Gate : June 3, 1809.

My dear Sir,—I have been so busy in forwarding our 2nd No.[3] that I have not been able to look to the right hand or the left. It is now out, and I am running away for a short time to the seaside to refresh my eyes and do nothing. I do not wonder that some objectionable passages are found in the first No. I see too many myself, but the allusion to the holy-water of the Mexican converts is an historical fact. But, in truth, there is vast room for

---

[1] Dean Ireland.   [2] Sir Walter.

[3] The allusions to a *Review* in these two letters refer to the *Quarterly,* which had only just come into existence under Gifford's auspices, and to the early numbers of which Hodgson contributed.

improvement ; and for this I am very anxious. Such articles as appear in some of the smaller reviews might be got by loads, but we aim at, or at least wish for, something better. That we shall succeed is, indeed, problematical ; but without it, it is quite certain that we might as well sit with our hands before us, and do nothing. It is not by common exertions that the ' Edinburgh Review' can be met, and the others are not objects of contention. To write panegyrics and satires is easy enough ; but this is not criticism : and I have already been obliged to omit more than I have inserted. From you, my dear Sir, I look for valuable assistance : for this, it will be necessary to put friendship out of the question, and to judge from established principles of the art. What has sunk the British critic but a base dereliction of all independence ? I know little of the other Reviews, but I suspect they do not flourish greatly—and from the same cause.

Lord Byron's poem[1] sales well I understand. I have an angry review of it, which I shall not use ; for though it is well written, it is manifestly unjust. Unless works can be made to amuse or instruct the reader, it is loss of time to dwell long on them or

---

[1] 'English Bards.'

indeed to dwell on them at all. 'Hesiod,' which is gone to your cousin,[1] may afford a neat article, but seems scarcely worth a long one. However, you will judge. I think, indeed, that almost all our articles are too long.

If success be a proof of merit (which it certainly is not) we might be vain ; for our second number is nearly out of print in the first three days. Yet we must look forward to something better.

Ever, my dear, Sir,

Your very faithful friend and servant,

WM. GIFFORD.

P.S. I leave town this morning for Ryde, in the Isle of Wight, where I shall remain for about six weeks, and where, as well as in every other place, I shall be glad to hear from you.

In the autumn of this year (1809) the public oratorship at Cambridge fell vacant, and Hodgson unsuccessfully contested it. His residence at Cambridge had hardly been long enough to entitle him to success, and Mr. Tatham, of St. John's, the successful candidate, had anticipated him in obtaining the votes of the most influential members of the Senate. Nevertheless, that Hodgson's claims were fully recognised

---

[1] John Hodgson, Esq., a barrister at Lincoln's Inn.

is proved by the complimentary letters which he received from many men of eminent distinction. Sir Vicary Gibbs, then Attorney-General, who had defeated Lord Palmerston in the preceding year in the representation of Cambridge, considered him eminently qualified for the office; Lord Palmerston himself wrote very courteously regretting that he had already promised to support Mr. Tatham, a member of his own college; Lords Euston, Clarendon, and Althorp, and H.R.H. The Duke of Gloucester wrote in a similar strain.

After this disappointment Hodgson again turned his thoughts to private tuition as an employment for his vacations. The following letter from Dr. Goodall, then head-master of Eton, is in answer to an application on this subject, and is written with the easy elegance which characterised that most dilettante of Dominies, who probably had slight suspicion that the young man whom he now addressed with such condescending kindliness, was destined to be his next successor in that provostship of Eton to which he himself was shortly to succeed.

Upper School, ex Cathedrâ : Nov. 14, 1809.

My dear Sir,—While half a hundred unwilling poets are labouring with all their might to draw off the spirit of the 32nd chapter of Deuteronomy, which they will most of them do very effectually in one sense at least, I have full leisure to acknowledge the receipt of your letter, and to say that I have little doubt of having occasional opportunities of assisting your views, which I shall most gladly embrace, but must consider the parents of the boys who may be fortunate enough to be your pupils as the persons obliged. I have unwittingly transferred the description of my own live stock to the sons of Alma Mater : I should certainly have said the young men. Would that I could have added my congratulations ! I am induced to think that only a nomination[1] was wanting.

Many thanks for your kind greetings. My Brethren must fully share with me whatever praise accrues from the present order of things at Eton.

Believe me to be with the truest regard,

My dear Sir,

Yours ever most faithfully,

J. GOODALL.

Considering the state of stagnation then prevailing at Eton Dr. Goodall's compliment to his colleagues must be regarded as of doubtful value.

---

[1] This, of course, refers to the public oratorship.

Among Hodgson's letters relating to this period there is one addressed to his father by an old friend, dated December 29, 1809, part of which is not without interest as throwing the light of contemporary opinion upon the state of public feeling on the war and its great instigator Bonaparte :—

I hope that this mild winter has been propitious to your health, as well as Mrs. Hodgson's. In this part of the world we have hitherto had nothing that deserves the name of winter. I wish I could say that the political season was as mild as the natural ; this, however, is by no means the case ; the political almanack makers prognosticate great changes: I fear that some of the Cabinet will fall victims to the *Walcheren typhus* ; but I am not yet convinced that it will kill the whole Cabinet : I presume there must be an inquiry, and perhaps the result of it may prove that our commanders adopted the most prudent, though not the most glorious, line of conduct. All sorts of changes are of course rumoured, but my opinion is that the Government will meet the question fairly. There is one diffi- culty, however (I think the principal one), which will unavoidably embarrass any administration, even a new one : *the war has spun out into great length, and the expenses of it bear heavily on most*

people. I had flattered myself that somehow or
other matters would have jumbled into something
like peace, but in this expectation I have indeed
been disappointed. Bonaparte seems, however,
disposed to enter on a more peaceable career, and,
after having so long been the universal destroyer of
mankind, to endeavour to make amends for the
ravages of his sword by a life of matrimonial usefulness. Of course he is to do great things in thirty
years, but I sincerely trust that, at any rate, he may
be disappointed in his wishes to preserve the crown
of France to the Corsican Dynasty, and that if he ever
should have a son, it may be taken from him as he
took away the unfortunate Duke d'Enghien. The
sister of the Emperor of Russia, who has already
refused him twice, is again the object of his choice.

In May of this year Byron invited his most intimate friends to Newstead for a last visit before his
departure from England, of which visit Charles
Skinner Matthews has given a graphic account; and
in June he addressed a farewell letter to Hodgson
from Falmouth with a spirited copy of verses quoted
by Moore, some of which, however, might have been
well omitted, as the vivacity and *verve* with which
they are written hardly compensate for their coarse-

ness. This remark applies equally to several passages in letters which were carefully marked for
omission by Hodgson, before being forwarded to
Moore, who had previously promised scrupulously to
regard Hodgson's wishes in this matter, but who could
not resist the temptation to insert everything which
would, in his opinion, directly or indirectly contribute
to the success of his work. It will be perceived that
such a proceeding was equally unfair to the writer and
to the recipient of these letters. Byron was very
young, only twenty-one, when they were written, and
was full of animal life and spirits. His innate love of
mischief, of shocking people's prejudices, and of representing himself as far more reckless and irreligious
than he really was, doubtless contributed to suggest
sentiments and modes of expression which his better
judgment would have condemned, and which no one
more deeply deplored than the person to whom they
were addressed.

For the two years of Byron's first absence from
England he corresponded constantly with Hodgson;
and some of this correspondence, hitherto unpub-
lished, but full of interest, will be found in the following pages.

At the beginning of the present chapter reference
was made to John Lonsdale, as being a contemporary

of Byron's at Cambridge, and as sharing with him Hodgson's friendship at that time. How sincere that friendship was is attested by the following lines, written by Hodgson at night in the stage coach, on his way to the Bury election. Lonsdale, in his youth, wrote poetry, but had the generosity and good sense to admire and appreciate at its proper value the genius of his brilliant companion.

> *Multa fides Plectri Sociis, et cara Sorori*
> *Multa Venus.*

Let warlike chiefs with envious eye
  Behold a brother's fame ;
Let close-leagued statesmen fairly vie
  To win the noblest name.
But, Lonsdale ! let not gentler minds
  Renounce their native pride,
That chain of love which firmly binds
  Our rival to our side.
Oh, thou hast loved the high-soul'd youth,
  Whose song transcended thine,
Nor heaved one sigh, to wrong the Truth
  That praised his glowing line.
Thy heart has beat, when friends around
  Rehearsed his rapturous lays,
True echoes to the noble sound
  That spoke thy rival's praise.
Thus oft on David's heav'nly lyre
  Hung Saul's enchanted son ;
Thus kindled, as the thrilling wire
  Their tuneful contest won.

Thus oft in Ovid's wondering ear
  Propertius' music flow'd ;
Thus o'er Tibullus' youthful bier
  Their mutual pity glow'd.
Thus Horace raised his Virgil's fame ;
  Thus, different far in mind,
Far humbler bards, in heart the same,
  Still love the tuneful kind.
The Muse with a magnetic force
  Attracts her genuine sons,
And each upon his crowded course
  With blameless ardour runs.
I dream not of the vulgar crew
  Who damn'd to deathless fame,
Their native dirt on Dryden threw,
  Or envied Pope his name.
Dumb scorn be theirs ! The faintest ray
  That Virtue darts within
Drives Envy's gathering clouds away,
  And banishes the sin.
How to his Gray's exalted height
  Did conscious Mason bend,
And, buried in that blaze of light,
  Still feel the bard his friend.
Yes, Lonsdale, yes, the friendly glow
  Is sweeter far than fame ;
Not only tuneful breasts below
  That generous feeling claim :
Oft have I seen the beauteous maid
  Admire a sister's grace,
And mark well-pleased the homage paid
  To her triumphant face.

And thus, methought, in realms above
  Rejoicing saints may see
Some tribute of angelic love
  To brighter purity.
Such thoughts be thine, my manly friend !
  Reject unworthy fear :
Some generous rival shall attend,
  And urge thy own career.
But haste to Life ! no glorious scope
  Can in these walls be found ;[1]
The grave of disappointed Hope
  Ambition's early bound.
Here Indolence with baneful frost
  Shall nip the vernal bloom ;
Here Shame shall mourn o'er glory lost,
  And Vice await its doom.
Haste, haste to Life ! Thy heart be zeal,
  Discretion be thy tongue ;
Grow old in honour quick, but feel
  In friendship ever young.

Dear Lonsdale,—The jolting of the Bury coach must palliate the roughness of the above. Think of what I say. But do not only think—act ! act !

  Dum res, et ætas, et Sororum
  Fila trium patiuntur atra.

If I am not at home (but I intend to be so at present) by 9 o'clock to-morrow night, say there will be no lectures on Tuesday.

Yours,   F. H.

[1] King's College.

CHAPTER VI.

LETTERS FROM HIS FATHER—POLITICAL ALLUSIONS
—IMPRISONMENT OF SIR FRANCIS BURDETT—
POLITICAL SQUIBS—LINES BY DENMAN—EPITAPH
FOR WINDHAM—FATHER'S DEATH.

1810.

IN the spring of the following year some letters, addressed to Hodgson at Cambridge by his father, contain sensible criticisms of current literature and politics.

Barwick : March 5, 1810.

My dear Frank,—We had been for some time expecting to hear from you, and therefore your letter by yesterday's post was received with much pleasure. Mr. Coke I should hope has some small chance of getting Gladestry. But the Chancellor[1] I understand is notorious both for making promises and breaking them.

I do not think the Walcheren inquiry will

[1] Lord Eldon.

turn the ministry out. The expedition was set
about too late, as indeed all our military schemes
always are ; but, considering the circumstances, as
much was done as could be expected. The loss of
so many men by sickness is the only thing to be
regretted. Lord Chatham was not the fittest
person to execute it ; his subsequent conduct is not
to be defended. So I give him up. The epigram [1]
is excellent.

I read the 'Monthly Review' some days ago,
and immediately recognised your hand in two of
the articles—the 'Persius' [2] and the 'Chatterton.'
They both are well done and do you credit. You
will say I am growing fastidious, for I do not admire
Dr. Ireland's learned book on Paganism, &c. At
this time of day such stale objections ought not to
be stirred. When Rome existed and was heathen
they might be proper, but not so now. They have
lost all their interest. The book, however, is a
proof of the various research and consummate judgment of the writer. The Westminster boys when
they heard it must have been amused if not edified

[1]   'The Earl of Chatham, with his sword drawn,
       Stood waiting for Sir Richard Strahan ;
       Sir Richard, longing to be at 'em,
       Stood waiting for the Earl of Chatham.'
[2]   Stowes's *Translation of Persius*.

by the lecturer. It was impossible for them to understand what he was about. I read it through with some attention, and admire very much the abstracts given from Austin and Cicero, and Varro, cum multis aliis et Græcis et Latinis. His observations on your note respecting Socrates[1] came from Mosheim and a sermon of Barrows; and they were well founded; but his expression that Socrates did not teach a *proper creation*, is a very improper one. Any writer less affected would have said, Socrates did not teach a creation properly so called; but ohe, jam satis.

. My time has been much engaged[2] of late in pursuing a gang of villains who have long infested Leeds and this neighbourhood. Eleven are already in York Castle, where I purpose going on Monday to be present at their trials, and to give some of them a good word to the judge; who I hope will be my old friend and schoolfellow, Sir Simon Le Blanc; we have not met since we parted in the year 1766 at the Charter House. We all join in our love, and a wish to hear from you soon.

Yours always,

J. HODGSON.

---

[1] Vide *supra*, p. 89.

[2] Mr. Hodgson was a very active magistrate.

From the same to the same.

Barwick: March 28, 1810.

My dear Son,—I have been for some days working myself up to a resolution to answer several letters of a much longer date than yours, but have taken you first, as a proof that you stand before all others in my thoughts and affection. Indeed you have put a question to me that rather required an earlier notice. Shall you go to Rugby this year, if the same office [1] is offered to you? Not if you are a loser by the honour. But I should think that might be remedied by a candid statement of the facts to your friend Dr. Wooll. The examiner ought to have a remuneration clear of all expenses. Then it would be an object worth seeking. This is my opinion; I leave you to judge if it is well founded. It has struck me that if Sir J. Cotterell could be prevailed on to apply to the Chancellor of the Exchequer for the living of Gladestry, the procrastinating Lord Eldon would be driven to a decision. I am sorry to be obliged to believe all the hard things you say of him; but he has certainly committed himself to such censure in too many instances.

[1] That of Classical Examiner of the Upper Forms.

Turning out Mr. York, for a silly boy, I certainly do not approve of. If his being unshaken in his attachment to the present Government be a fault, it surely is a venial one; and if his being rewarded for it is blameable, I suspect there are not many who would not gladly submit to the same blame on the same account. Mr. York is a man of character, of family, and of considerable talents, and must be respectable, whether he is your county member, or for any petty borough. The epigram on 'Gratia gratiam parit' is very fair. Mr. Bull must be excused in all his absurdities for the sake of his old Whig principles. But what think you of Lord Erskine and Mr. Clifford, and their wish to exclude from the bar all persons engaged in periodical papers? Such an infamous project was never heard of; but it may be forgiven, if for no better reason, than from having been the occasion of that noble burst of eloquence from Mr. Stephens and Sheridan. The 'Battle of Falkirk' I have not yet seen, but my longing is increased both by your remarks and those of the 'Critical Review.' The translation [1] of the 'Georgics,' which are noticed in the last 'Monthly Review,' I have no sort of wish

[1] Stawell and Deare's.

to know more of. I more than suspect I know the critic.

I am glad to hear Mr. Bland is doing well at Amsterdam. In these fearful times the ministers of the Church have a difficult task to perform, in an enemy's country, with an unsettled Government. I augur favourably from the union between Bonaparte and the Austrian princess. It may lead to that which the sword could never bring to pass. I saw my old schoolfellow Le Blanc at York, and was cordially recognised by him at a large party to whom he gave a dinner. We returned to our boyish days, and he seemed pleased with the recollection of our former intimacy. As a judge he is far above my praise. Such mildness in expounding the laws, and such firmness in enforcing them, gave me a very high opinion of his head and heart. My villains, at least six of them, are sentenced to transportation for seven years ; but, in order to convict them, it was found necessary to admit four of them as evidence.

The Edinburgh severe tribunal has passed sentence on our present Ministers with such diabolical malice, and has given such an alarming picture of the evils it supposes to be impending, that were it to obtain credit it would be impossible to go to our beds with any degree of comfort or security. But are we to judge of the state of affairs from the factious babbling of a Waithman or a Wardle, or the intemperate and ill-informed opinions of young partisans, or from the general demeanour of the majority of the public? They seem to be perfectly satisfied that the State is not going to ruin; nor can they be otherwise when they see a disposition in their rulers to reform all abuses, to correct all unnecessary expenditure, to encourage commerce and agriculture, and whatever tends to improve and enrich the country; above all, when they see the laws so impartially and so promptly executed, and even-handed justice protecting and punishing all persons without favour or distinction, according to their merits. If dinner had not been announced I could have improved the panegyric by entering on a detail of the meritorious services of Mr. Perceval, Lord Castlereagh, and Lord Chatham.

I am ever, dear Frank, yours,

JAMES HODGSON.

From the same to the same.

Barwick: April 26, 1810.

My dear Son,—I have been so very unwell for the last fortnight as to have been in some degree

obliged to defer till now making an acknowledgment of your last letter. . . . . Thank you for the
epigrams ! Your pupil room, under the auspices of
two such demigods,[1] must be the ipsissimus locus
scientiæ et sapientiæ. In answer to your query
respecting Butler's 'Analogy,' I will transcribe a note
which I made many years ago, and which stands
now in the first blank page of Archbishop Secker's
Sermons, vol. i. 'The merit of these sermons con-
sists in explaining, clearly and popularly, the principles delivered by Butler in his famous book of
the "Analogy," &c., and in showing the important
use of them to religion.' Upon this I observed at
the time : 'This remark applies more particularly
to Secker's first three sermons, vol. i.'

Dr. Burney of Greenwich has lately published
an abbreviated edition of 'Pearson on the Creed.'
Perhaps it may be more readable than the original.
After all, the book, the whole book, is aureum opus.

I lament your separation from the 'Quarterly
Review,' because the last two numbers have given
me a high opinion of the writers in it. Dr. Ireland
has shown his transcendent abilities in more than
one article if I am not mistaken. I have not seen
the last 'Monthly,' and therefore cannot say anything

[1] Locke and Pearson.

of its merits. But I should imagine one Review quite enough for one critic. It pleases me much to hear you speak so handsomely of Mr. Griffiths.[1]

I am happy to add your mother is getting better. She has been out once in the carriage, and we are going again to-day to call on the new proprietors of Parlington, Mr. and Mrs. Oliver Gascoigne.

We all join in love and best wishes,

Yours always,

J. HODGSON.

From the same to the same.

Barwick: May 16, 1810.

My dear Frank,—Only six days you will please to take notice from the date of your last, for which habeo gratias. Certainly Terence, if he did not write better plays than Plautus, &c., wrote his own language with greater purity and elegance. I know he was called 'dimidiate Menander,' but a nick-name may imply excellence as well as defect.

I have not, indeed, been engaged in reviewing essays upon Plato, but I have been re-reviewing certain manuscripts that once a week are submitted to our village critics. This morning, indeed, I have

[1] Editor of the *Monthly*.

been deep in the 'Monthly,' and much pleased with the first article, Maurice's translation of the 'Iliad.' The critic [1] seems to be no ordinary hand, and to be well acquainted with the different merits of rhyme and blank verse. I was glad to perceive he had a good opinion of Cowper's talents in general, though no admirer of his 'Homer.' But I do not agree as to the pompous inanity of the author of the 'Task.' Crabbe I have not read, and for the present feel satisfied with the copious extracts in the 'Review.' I had almost let slip Homer's astronomical simile, of the correctness of which I once was convinced by the remark of a countryman, a carpenter I believe. 'Mrs. Plunkett' I shall certainly not cut, if uncut; and if cut, I shall not open. Marsh's letter I have sent for. He cannot exercise the lash too severely on a set of scoundrels who set no bounds to their imposture. I agree with you entirely as to the absurdity of our very learned Doctors shooting over the heads of their readers and hearers. But stripped of their fine dress, I suspect they would lose some of their admirers. But what is so useful or so attractive as plain sense in plain language! Warburton I have read, and thought him, when intelligible, a very superior writer.

[1] This was Francis Hodgson.

There was an excellent critique on the correspondence between him and Bishop Hurd in one of the last Quarterly Reviews. ' Hyloe ' was the name of one of Bishop Berkeley's dialogues on the non-existence of matter out of the mind. Such reasonings are not substantial enough for me. Dr. Burney's edition of Pearson seems to be like spoiling a pudding by taking the plums out of it.

The political ferment of the last month is, from the proper firmness of the Ministry, beginning to subside. The extreme party seem at last to be aware of the mischief that must arise from indiscriminate abuse. Wardle and Waithman would never have taken such liberties, had not Windham and Whitbread set them the example. Mr. Ponsonby, the vir pietate gravis ac meritis, hath amply redeemed all past perverseness by his admirable speech. As for Sir Francis,[1] yet a little while and he will be forgotten. His tutor blames, it is said, his late conduct. But this I much doubt. Deportation will probably be the fate of some of these worthies, if they renew their machinations. The thieves I committed to York, and who are now lying in the hulks, are to be sent off to South Wales[2] by the first conveyance. This is the last

[1] Burdett.   [2] New South Wales.

favour I could show them for expressing publicly
their wish to return to Barwick, for no other purpose than that of murdering me and two or three
others.   But are these men so bad as Burdett and
Company ?

      We all join in wishing you health and happiness.

                                    Yours,

                              JAMES HODGSON.

In the preceding month Francis Hodgson had received a letter from his cousin, John Hodgson, of
Lincoln's Inn, which contains a vivid description of
the imprisonment of Sir Francis Burdett.

                        Lincoln's Inn : April 9, 1810.

My dear Frank,—The review of Anstey's works is at
length completed ; I hope it will make ten or
twelve pages, but it has been written piecemeal and
amidst many interruptions, and I cannot pride
myself much upon it However, such as it is,
Griffiths shall have it to-night or to-morrow.   You
have, of course, seen how civil the 'Critical' has
been to you.

      Sir Francis Burdett was taken to the Tower
this morning.   As he had repeatedly declared,
both publicly and privately, that he would not
surrender, it was necessary to resort to force.

His house was accordingly invested this morning, between nine and ten, by a large party of civil officers, headed by the Sergeant-at-Arms, and backed by a very strong military guard ; and, admission being refused, the door was broken open, and the windows on the first floor scaled. He made no personal resistance, and was therefore conveyed into a carriage, and, attended by a regiment of Horse Guards, was safely lodged in the Tower. As the Guards passed through Fenchurch Street and that neighbourhood the mob grew so troublesome and insulting that they were obliged to fire, and a sort of skirmishing took place, in which one man was killed, and some others wounded. When the service was performed the Guards left the City by the way of London Bridge. I long very much to see the Tower with its ditch filled, guns mounted, drawbridge up, &c. ; I hear it looks quite grand.

I cannot quite agree in your opinions of this business. With respect to the commitment of Gale Jones, although I am rather surprised at the existence of such a power, I cannot see any ground to dispute it. All text writers of every age acknowledge it, the most liberal and constitutional judges have uniformly approved of it, and the precedents are as old as there are journals of the House, and

the earliest of them speak of the power as one of
the undoubted privileges of the House of Commons.
Nor do I see any indiscretion in the exercise of the
power in Jones's case: he was by his own confes-
sion guilty, and the publication was of a mischie-
vous tendency.   His detention in prison is entirely
owing to his refusal to make a proper apology to
the House and to petition for his discharge.   With
respect to Sir Francis himself, he had admitted
the power of the House to commit one of its own
members; and surely when they had resolved that
his letter was a libel, it was too gross a one to merit
anything but the highest punishment they could
inflict.   It would have been better in my opinion
if neither of these absurd publications had been
noticed at all; but, as they were noticed, the House
was bound to maintain its dignity, and vindicate its
ancient and established rights and privileges.

The riots have been very considerable, especially
on Saturday night when the Horse Guards were
obliged to be very active, and some blood was certainly spilt, but I do not think it clear that any life
was lost till this morning.   Cannon were planted in
Soho, Bloomsbury, and Lincoln's Inn Squares, and
quite a park of artillery opposite the offender's
house in Piccadilly.   I understand   there   are

fourteen thousand troops in London. Meantime Bonaparte is getting happily married and settled at Paris.

Let me hear from you soon; and believe. me dear Frank, yours very affectionately,

JOHN HODGSON.

On another occasion Sir Francis Burdett was conveyed by river to avoid the mob—an event which suggested to Hodgson the following political squib, to which are appended some lines on other political agitators of the period.

THE PATRIOTS. A CANTATA.

RECITATIVE.

Her ladyship sits in Wimbledon bower
To see her dear lord return from the Tower,
With the merry merry cleavers' jocund tone,
And the merry merry sound of the marrow-bone.
But Sir Francis returns another way,
For thus to him Lord Moira did say :

Air—'Begone, dull Care.'

' Begone, Burdett ! I prithee begone from me ;
Begone, Burdett, as soon as you've paid your fee !

(*Aside with deep reflection.*)

The Speaker may dance, and the Serjeant may sing,
So merrily pass the day ;
For I've held it always the wisest thing
To row Burdett away.'

RECITATIVE.

Mrs. Waithman behind the counter doth sit
    A-measuring out the linen so nice.
But where is her mate, 'the terror of Pitt?'
    He's giving the councilmen good advice.

    Air—'Oh, the joys beyond expression!'

'Oh, the joys of speechifying!
    Oh, the rapture mouthing brings!
Idly raving, basely lying,
    Damning laws, insulting kings.
Oh, how blest the linendraper
    Who all day makes speeches bright—
And in the " Statesman," moderate paper,
    Reads them o'er again at night!'

RECITATIVE.

Mrs. Jones is placed at the British Forum
To welcome her Gale with due decorum ;
For no longer in Newgate must he stay,
And they've turn'd him out of his lodging to-day ;
They've turn'd him out ere his friends approach,
And whipp'd him off in a hackney coach.

    Air—'Strawberry Hill.'

'Let others praise Mac'ullum,
    And Dodd and Glennie tell ;
But little folks love John Gale Jones,
    Love John Gale Jones as well.
With some men Hague and Hogan
    May bear away the bell,
But not a patriot in the town
    Doth John Gale Jones excel,' &c.

Denman, writing about the same time, encloses some characteristic lines on a recent election.

'Tis over ! This tool of contractors and knaves—
This hireling of hirelings—this servant of slaves—
Despised in our heart and condemn'd by our voice—
Must be sent to the House as *the man of our choice.*
The defender of all for which Britain should fight,
The gallant young champion of freedom and right,
Whom each eye greets with gladness, each bosom admires,
Overpower'd, not subdued, from the contest retires.
What heart so devoted to fortune can be,
What heart so abandoned, oh Glory, by thee,
As to hug the dishonour which vict'ry makes sweet,
And prefer such a triumph to such a defeat ?
The event for a moment let patriots deplore—
Let liberty droop for a moment—no more !
Her rights basely ravish'd she soon shall reclaim,
Her force unabated, her spirit the same.
Thro' each generous bosom that spirit shall spread,
When all the vile arts that opposed it are dead,
When duty and shame at corruption shall spurn,
And insulting oppression make cowardice turn, &c.

A letter of yours came yesterday ; another this morning, enclosing one which I immediately despatched to Richmond. You may depend on my going there as soon as the numberless little but necessary things which the election has put out of my head are tolerably got through. What a strange, divided state the Hugonots are got into !

The great general denomination will, I fear, be broken into a variety of sects, Pædobaptists, Independents, Millenarians, &c. I am a good deal disposed in my own mind to the scheme of the Fifth Monarchy. But you, who talk of gloominess and solitude and consequent despondency, how enviable must your situation be, with Paley and Bland, whom you will see before or soon after this letter, in your immediate neighbourhood! I hope there is a half-way house, and shall picture to myself a beautiful little cottage covered with straggling vines, and surrounded with a large rambling sort of garden, &c.

Just before the long vacation Hodgson wrote to his father enclosing some verses on Windham.

Cambridge : June 15, 1810.

My dear Father,—I am quite ashamed to see the distance between the date of your last letter and that of the present. But I should have written much sooner had I not wished to give you an account of a visit which my uncle and cousins have been paying me at Cambridge. They came on Saturday and went away on Wednesday last. The time passed very pleasantly in examining halls, and chapels, and libraries ; some of which sights were new even to myself. On the last day they had an opportunity of hearing of a pretty severe display of university discipline ; for the stern Calvinist of Queen's, Dr. Milner, expelled four young men for certain irregularities, which have passed for some years with reprehension much less rigorous. The party seemed much pleased with their visit ; and I was very glad to have an opportunity of showing them the lions.

What a strange mysterious business the attempt to assassinate the Duke of Cumberland—but what a loss the public have had in Windham ! Great and good as he was, he would have been missed in any times, but in the present his death is a general calamity. Some of the attendants upon his funeral, which took place at Felbrig, passed through this town yesterday. Surely he should have been buried in Westminster Abbey ! The thought struck me so forcibly that I prepared an epitaph for him, which I transcribe for you below. Tell me if you think it is tolerable : worthy of its subject I am aware it is not.

EPITAPH FOR WINDHAM.

Ye sacred stones, by English mourners prest,
Where Fox and Chatham's son in concord rest,

Open your vaults, and at their honour'd side
Place the third prop of England's falling pride.
What worthy claimant of this hallow'd tomb
Lives yet to check his country's awful doom ?
Close, close your vaults, ye stones, for ever close,
Where glory's last Triumvirate repose.
Oh ! timely call'd to share the patriot's grave,
Nor see the ruin'd State thou couldst not save.
Windham, adieu ! by all the good approved,
By Johnson honour'd, and by Burke beloved,
In Truth's decay to high-soul'd Virtue true,
Thou setting star of ancient Fame, adieu !
What prescient terrors at thy loss arise !
What tears of sorrow fill Reflection's eyes !
Who now remains, with treasured Learning fraught,
To wake like thee the teeming world of thought ?
Who now remains in rival ardour strong,
To roll the tide of eloquence along ?
Prompt at thy call creative Fancy came,
And Reason bore thee on her wings of flame :
Fancy unfelt by Slavery's venal crew,
Reason too bright for Dulness' owlet view.
Rejoin, blest shade, the sons of Genius fled,
And swell the synod of the virtuous dead.
Revered companion of the good and wise,
Rejoin thy loved precursors in the skies.

I am glad you like the review of 'Maurice.'
That of the 'Minstrels of Acre,' and of 'Wallace,' in
the last month, were also mine.   Look in future for
Christie's 'Etruscan Vases,' Girdlestone's 'Pindar,'
Butler's 'Æschylus,' and Drummond's 'Hercula-

nensia;' and Walter Scott's 'Lady of the Lake.' A noble poem!

My lectures are over, and my brother tutor has arrived. But I shall stay here till commencement, working at my reviews. This will be the first week in July; and I shall then accompany a college friend, who drives me across country to Harrow. From thence I shall turn my face northwards, and, getting into some 'leathern convenience' at Barnet, shall early in August, I hope, reach Barwick. Friends in London are quite well again. May this letter find you, my mother and sister,[1] in health and spirits! The blessing of the latter I begin to feel more sensibly every day. Singula de nobis anni prædantur euntes. Adieu, **my dear father!** With kindest love ever yours,

F. H.

The Latin quotation in the last sentence of this letter was unconsciously prophetic. In accordance with his intention, mentioned above, Francis Hodgson spent the greater part of his vacation at Barwick, and on the day of his departure for Cambridge his father, having seen him off by the coach from Leeds, sat on the bench as a magistrate, and, on his return to Bar-

---

[1] 'Married to her cousin the Rev. G. F. Coke, and died young.

wick in the evening of the same day, died quite suddenly of heart disease.   His character is sketched in
outline in a letter of condolence addressed by an old
and favourite pupil, Cecil Jenkinson, afterwards Lord
Liverpool, to his friend and former companion Francis
Hodgson.

Ditchford Hall: October 20, 1810.

My dear Frank,—I received the melancholy news
conveyed to me by your letter the day before
yesterday, and should have expressed to you my
feelings sooner had not a particular engagement on
that day, and the circumstance of the post not going
out yesterday from Shrewsbury, prevented me from
so doing.   It is impossible for me to express to
you how much I lament the event which has deprived you of a kind and affectionate father, and
myself of an old, sincere, and valued friend.   My
obligations to your father are so well known to you
that, was it not for fear of the accusation of ingrati-
tude, it would be needless for me to mention them
in this place.   From the period of time which was
passed by me at sea my education would have been
deplorable had I not received from him that foster-
ing aid and assistance which enabled me to appear
at the university little inferior in my classical
studies to those whose education had been con-

ducted by the more certain and regular process of
public education. His manner of instruction was
not the least part of the obligation I owe your
father; he inspired me with that desire of knowledge which alone enabled me to make the rapid
progress I did. I must beg that you will at a
proper moment convey to your mother those feelings of sorrow which I have attempted but faintly
to express. It would be, I am sure, unnecessary
for me to tell you that my attachment to your
father will be remembered by me towards those
whom he has left behind. I hope, if your avocations call you at any time either towards this
county or London, that you will favour me with a
visit, and that you will believe that you can never
have a more sincere or affectionate friend than

CECIL JENKINSON.

This sudden and unexpected death involved
Francis Hodgson in serious pecuniary difficulties.
His father had held successively the livings of
Humber in Herefordshire, of Keston in Kent, of
South-Repps in Norfolk, and lastly of Barwick-in-
Elmet in Yorkshire, besides having been minister of
the Savoy Chapel in the Strand, and chaplain to
Lords Hawksbury and Dunmore. The frequent re-

movals which these several preferments entailed had occasioned considerable expenses, and the rectory house and grounds at Barwick had recently undergone various important alterations and improvements. The rector, moreover, had long been accustomed to exercise open-handed liberality to his poorer parishioners, and, in anticipation of his future ample capabilities of repayment of loans, had left out of sight the uncertainty of life. Francis Hodgson at once determined to discharge all his father's debts— an undertaking which for some years continued to embarrass him, until the extraordinary generosity of his friend, Lord Byron, placed him once more in a position of independence.

CHAPTER VII.

CONTRIBUTIONS TO REVIEWS—EARLY POEMS— LINES TO BYRON.

1811.

HAVING previously engaged to contribute to the
'Monthly' and 'Critical' Reviews, Hodgson was
reluctantly compelled to terminate his connection
with the 'Quarterly' after the publication of its first
few numbers. The similarity of the subjects discussed, and the arduousness of his other avocations,
rendered this step necessary, although the almost
immediate success of the 'Quarterly' must have
made such a step doubly distasteful. · But in the
'Critical' and 'Monthly' Reviews of this period
nearly all the articles on classical subjects, and very
many others on English and French literature, were
written by Hodgson, and display impartial criticism,
an extensive and profound erudition, and a correct,
cultivated taste. Girdlestone's edition of the 'Odes'
of Pindar, for instance ; Butler's 'Æschylus' and

'Musæ Cantabrigienses' were thoroughly congenial subjects, while two extremely learned and diffusely interesting essays on recent discoveries at Herculaneum and on Christie's 'Etruscan Vases' prove the minuteness of his archæological and philological researches.

In the article on the 'Musæ Cantabrigienses' there are some curious criticisms of contemporary scholarship at Cambridge. The early effusions of the great Dr. Keate are there characterised by his old pupil as 'boyish;' but it is also admitted that a bold and original spirit pervades his poems, and that, if they be not correctly classical in their flow, they must be forgiven for their unborrowed harmony and for that first of poetical virtues—

> Wild Nature's vigour stirring at the root.

But while Dr. Keate is pronounced to possess more fire than any other contributor, both he and Dr. Butler are found guilty of a fault which, to modern head-masters, will appear sufficiently astonishing. Each of them, more than once, uses a final vowel short before 'sp' and 'sc'! The ode of C. J. Blomfield (afterwards Bishop of London) on the assassination of the Duc d'Enghien, is declared to be below criticism. 'Who but his French assassins,' it is asked, 'could have been guilty of such rudeness as to put such language into the mouth of that unfortunate prince.'

But the Greek ode of this poet is said to redeem his Latin peccadilloes, and he is understood to be a very promising scholar of Trinity College. Other contributors are commemorated as follows: J. Lonsdale, of King's College, 1807, elegantly and forcibly bewails the death of Pitt. Rennell's (King's College, 1808) Greek ode on 'Spring' is a very spirited and elegant production ; and Joseph Goodall, the present Provost of Eton, commemorates the earthquake in the West Indies, in an ode dated 1781, with much poetic spirit ; while of the epigrams, the 'Bellus Homo Academicus,' by the last-named author, both in Latin and Greek, is tame mediocrity—one of those cheap displays of wisdom which nobody values because everybody possesses it, yet, in point of expression, these are perhaps two of the best in the epigrammatic collection. Keate on a 'Donkey Race,' ὕστερον πρότερον, is not bad. Frere on a 'Dumb Beggar' is excellent. B. Drury on the 'Mutilated Statue of Ceres' demands praise. Silence best describes the rest.

In his review on 'An Essay on Plato by M. Combe-Dounous,' Hodgson writes a masterly vindication of

Christianity against the attacks of the French sceptic, who professes a preference for Platonism, and who, like other infidels, 'proudly limits the power of the Creator by the creature's ignorance.' At the conclusion of his essay M. Dounous explains the extraordinary influence of early Christianity by an astonishing assertion, ' Le sage Hébreu s'etait attaché des disciples parmi les lettres de sa nation,' and is thus answered by his reviewer :—

Arise in judgment against your false historian, ye poor and humble propagators of the Gospel of Christ, and bid him blush for that philosophy which can condescend to advocate its cause by unmanly misrepresentations. Who but St. Paul was learned among you? Who were the deep and plotting philosophers, who, after the death of their Master, met at Jerusalem to lay the doctrines of Plato, and Pythagoras, and Zeno under contribution; and by this eclectic method to form a syncretism of moral and religious opinions for the learned, and of prodigies and miracles for the vulgar? Where is the record, the history, the hint of such a proceeding? Who were the actors in this drama? What secondary causes, in a word, supposing all the unwarrantable assertions of this fanatic Platonist (for in charity we must suppose

that he is an enthusiast) to be true, will account
for the promulgation of Christianity? The speech
of Gamaliel has never been and can never be
answered: 'If this counsel or this work be of men,
it will come to nought; but if it be of God, ye
cannot overthrow it.' It is melancholy, indeed,
that this clever and learned Frenchman, whose
style is so superior, should have perverted his
distinguished talents to so malignant an attempt
as the substitution of the wild chimeras of Platonism, the ignis fatuus of pagan philosophy, for
the clear and steady light of Christianity.

On English literature Hodgson's reviews are so
numerous and extensive as to render even the most
partial reproduction impossible; but there are a few
concluding remarks in that one which treats of Scott's
'Lady of the Lake,' which, from the world-wide
celebrity of the poem, and from the interest which
belongs to contemporary criticism, may well be quoted
here. The various imitators of Scott, who copied his
style without sharing his genius, are mentioned with
becoming severity. Numerous verbal and gramma-
tical lapses are pointed out, and are attributed to the
glowing haste with which the poem was composed;
and then, after many eulogistic remarks expressive of

enthusiastic admiration for the poet's genius, Hodgson concludes his critique by saying :—

We may just observe that the notes contain some amusing stories, with others that are dull, and shall now take our leave of Mr. Scott, expressing a most sincere wish that his farewell address to his harp may not be more serious than the farewell addresses of poets usually are ; and adding that we hope our specified objections to parts of his poem, whether they be faults in the conduct of the plot, or inaccuracies of diction, will induce his numerous imitators at least to pause ere they contribute further to the wide corruption of our taste which is occasioned by such servility. We wish that we might reasonably hope that their great original himself, animated by the noble hope of living in the praises of posterity, would, even now, in the full tide of his present fame, lend an ear to our admonitions. Then might he soar like his own eagle,[1] and silence all his contemporaries.

Hodgson's first original poems were published in 1809, under the title 'Lady Jane Grey, a Tale in Two Books, with Miscellaneous Poems in English and Latin,' which were, on the whole, very favourably

---

[1] *Lady of the Lake*, canto iii. 55-60.

received by the public and the press. After alluding with some asperity to the satire on some of the reviewers of the translation of Juvenal, mentioned in a former chapter, the 'Critical' with singular generosity declares :—

For ourselves, we have always been, and still are, Mr. Hodgson's friends, however he may despise our goodwill ; willingly, therefore, we dismiss his satire from our recollection, and pass to a more grateful subject, the gentle Lady Jane.

A comparison follows with the 'Force of Religion; or, Vanquished Love,' by Dr. Young.

The subject is indeed very differently treated by the two poets. The plan adopted by Mr. Hodgson has one great advantage over that of the earlier author, since, by carrying back the scene to those hours of peace and love which were passed by Lady Jane in company with her books and her beloved Dudley, before the fatal ambition of a father had involved her in the final miseries of her existence, he has not only gained the advantage of much natural and pleasing description and many moral reflections of a stamp less awfully affecting than those to which the sad catastrophe of the tale gives occasion, but has likewise obtained those more technical benefits which the skilful artist knows how to derive from the force of contrast and the various emotions of the mind. The character, too, of his principal personage is much more truly and more beautifully represented by exhibiting it both in the lights and shades of life. . . . In the execution of his task it is safe to affirm that Mr. H. has most decidedly surpassed his predecessor ; and this not only in the superior ease and correctness of his versification, but also in the grace of his descriptions and the pathetic sentiments and reflections with which he has diversified and adorned his narrative.

'Dignified' and 'elegant' are the epithets applied by the 'Monthly' to 'Sir Edgar,' which it considers to be remarkable for a pleasing solemnity both of thought and cadence.

The rest of these volumes, which is made up of short poems on various subjects, and translations of the classics, is said to exhibit something not very unlike the inside of the study of a statuary or painter, which usually contains a whimsical collection of fragments and sketches, of designs half executed and then thrown aside, of forms just struggling for deliverance from the marble, or ready to start into life from the darkness of the canvas. Songs, tales, rhapsodies, fragments of letters, elegies amorous and moral, parodies, ballads, translations, burlesques, sonnets, epitaphs, epigrams, imitations, all follow each other in gay confusion.

But if [adds the reviewer] the severer order of critics may condemn the total absence of arrangement and connection apparent in the formation of this motley group, those who are more indulgent may pardon the author in consideration of the superior amusement which the reader will derive from this very want of order. Mr. Hodgson literally appears to think in verse,[1] and to set down every thought in his book as fast as it occurs to his imagination. But all whose minds are in any degree imbued with the same love of rhyme and the same variety of fancy which distinguished the author, will follow him with infinitely more satisfaction than they would the gravest and most methodical of his lecturers. Many of these poems exhibit uncommon powers of versification, and a fancy strongly occupied by all those enchanting impossibilities which

[1]   Sponte suâ carmen numeros veniebat ad aptos,
         Et quod tentabam dicere versus erat.
                          Ovid, *Trist. Eleg.* x. 25, 26.

are peculiarly the inheritance of the poet. The forms of gaiety, and mirth, and love, of melancholy, and madness, and despair, are hastily summoned and speedily dismissed ; they come like shadows, so depart ; but there is something desultory and impatient in Mr. Hodgson's poetical temperament which must be corrected if he would do himself justice, and would reach that high degree of excellence for which he appears to be destined. He has exercised himself long enough in morsels and fragments. We hope to see him engage in designs of greater magnitude, and try his powers of invention on a larger scale and by more continuous efforts.

Of 'An Answer to the Question of a Critic,' the 'Critical Review' writes :—

If any inducement were wanting to treat Mr. Hodgson in the most liberal spirit of criticism, the following excellent criticism of his own would supply us with it :—

> Where lies the charm ungovern'd Scott displays ?
> In the wild vigour of his lawless lays—
> And sudden bursts of tenderness are there,
> And warlike valour's animating air ;
> Castle and convent fill the glowing scene,
> Rocks tow'r around, and rivers roll between ;

The deeds of other days entranced we see,
Heraldic pomp, and pride of chivalry ;
The plundering inroad, the tumultuous fight,
Hail ! minstrel, feast, fair dame, and gallant knight.

Of the shorter poems in this collection two were addressed to Lord Byron immediately before his first departure from England. The concluding lines of the former contain timely admonitions respecting religion, elicited, doubtless, by previous conversations and correspondence : the latter appeals to the poet's sense of responsibility as an hereditary legislator. After a comparison between England and various foreign countries, and an allusion to the duties of patriotism, the first poem continues :—

> Yet if pleasing change allure thee
>   O'er the roughly swelling tide,
> May the one great Guide secure thee—
>   Byron, ne'er forget thy Guide.
>
> Mark Him, in the whirlwind riding,
>   O'er the darken'd billows sweep ;
> Mark Him, through the calm air gliding,
>   Bid th' obedient ocean sleep.
>
> See Him fill yon arch of Heav'n,
>   Glitt'ring with the gems of night ;
> See, nor hope to be forgiv'n
>   Doubtful of His sacred light.

See Him spread, in bright profusion,
  Varied wealth o'er ev'ry land;
See, nor rest in blind delusion,
  Doubtful of His bounteous hand.

But, if Nature fail to move thee
  With her rich external charms,
Raise thy thoughts to Him above thee
  From thy conscious soul's alarms.

Feel that soul's most deep recesses
  Touch'd by inspiration's pen ;
Feel, nor trust in impious guesses
  Of the thankless sons of men.

Then as o'er the midnight ocean
  Moves thy steady bark along,
On the deck, in calm devotion,
  Breathe to Heav'n thy secret song.

With the pure and holy feeling,
  Friendship in thy breast shall rise ;
And Remembrance, o'er thee stealing,
  Softly paint thy native skies.

ENERGY.

Byron ! since rank's discordant tone
  Allows the friendly sound—
Byron ! in energy alone
  Can genuine bliss be found.
He who exerts his native powers
  Can ne'er be long deprest ;

Young hope shall chide his loit'ring hours,
  Glad triumph cheer his breast ;
But hope, but triumph far have fled
  From love's despondent slave,
Whose dream of rhapsody is dead
  In disappointment's grave.
Oh ! then awake to glory's voice,
  Last of thy noble line !
Be eloquent renown thy choice,
  Be tuneful sorrow mine.
'Mid listening senates boldly stand
  Thy country's firm support—
Foe to rude faction's slavish band,
  And flattery's slaves at court.

This appeal received a satisfactory answer in that eloquent speech upon the Frame-Breaking Bill, of which the speaker sent the first account to his no less wise than considerate mentor, Francis Hodgson.

CHAPTER VIII.

1811.

THE letters written by Byron during his first pilgrimage, to which reference has been already made, are not less remarkable for keen observation and genial good-humour, than for that morbid self-consciousness which was their author's bane throughout his life. Some few sentences in the first of these letters give the key-note to many of the others, which are written with a racy freshness strangely belying some of the melancholy and misanthropic sentiments expressed in them. The date of this first letter is Lisbon, July 16, 1809.

Thus far have we pursued our route, and seen all
sorts of marvellous sights, palaces, convents, &c. ;
which, being to be heard of in my friend Hobhouse's

forthcoming 'Book of Travels,' I shall not anticipate by giving any account to you in a private and clandestine manner. I must just observe that the village of Cintra, in Estremadura, is the most beautiful, perhaps, in the world—very far superior to my expectation—and Portugal pleasant enough. The inhabitants have few vices, &c. ... The first and sweetest spot in this kingdom is Montserrat, lately the seat of the great Beckford.[1]

Hodgson! send me the news, and Hobby's Missellingany, and the deaths and defeats, and capital crimes, and the misfortunes of one's friends, and the controversies and criticisms. All this will be pleasant, suave mari magno, &c. Talking of that, I have been sea-sick and sick of the sea. Adieu!

Alluding to these Spanish letters, Byron writes to Drury when on board the ' Salsette ' frigate on his way from Smyrna to Constantinople.

Of Spain I sent some account to our Hodgson, but have subsequently written to no one save notes to relations and lawyers to keep them out of my premises. I mean to give up all connection, on my return, with many of my best friends, as I supposed them, and to snarl all my life. But I hope to have

---

[1] The millionaire; author of *Vathek*, and other works.

one good-humoured laugh with you, and to embrace Dwyer and pledge Hodgson before I commence cynicism.... Remember me to Claridge if not translated to college, and present to Hodgson assurances of my high consideration.

On the same voyage, when in the Dardanelles off Abydos, he writes to Hodgson a letter, extracts from which, although already in part published by Moore, will bear repetition.

I am on my way to Constantinople after a tour through Greece, Epirus, &c., and part of Asia Minor, some particulars of which I have just communicated to our friend and host H. Drury. With these, then, I shall not trouble you; but, as you will perhaps be pleased to hear that I am well, &c., I take the opportunity of our ambassador's return to forward the few lines I have time to despatch....

I have lived a good deal with the Greeks, whose modern dialect I can converse in enough for my purposes. With the Turks I have also some male acquaintances; female society is out of the question. I have been very well treated by the Pashas and Governors, and have no complaint to make of any kind. Hobhouse will one day inform you of all our adventures. Were I to attempt the recital,

neither *my* paper nor *your* patience would hold out
during the operation. Nobody save yourself has
written to me since I left England ; but, indeed, I
did not request it. I except my relations, who write
quite as often as I wish.   Of Hobhouse's volume
I know nothing, except that it is out ; and of my
second edition I do not even know *that*, and certainly do not, at this distance, interest myself in
the matter.   My friend H. is naturally anxious on
the head of his rhymes, which I think will succeed,
or at least deserve success; but he has not yet
acquired the 'calm indifference' (as Sir Fretful has
it) of *us old authors*. I hope you and Bland roll
down the stream of sale with rapidity, and that
you have produced a new poem.

Of my return I cannot positively speak, but
think it probable Hobhouse will precede me in
that respect. We have been very nearly one year
abroad. I should wish to gaze away another at least
in these evergreen climates, but I fear business—
law business, the worst of employments—will recall
me previous to that period, if not very quickly.
If so, you shall have due notice.   I am very serious
and cynical, and a good deal disposed to moralise ;
but, fortunately for you, the coming homily is cut
off by default of pen, and defection of paper.

Good morrow! If you write, address to me at Malta, whence your letters will be forwarded. You need not remember me to anybody, but believe me yours with all faith,

BYRON.

The postscript to this letter, which has never hitherto been published, was written on May 15, 1810, immediately after his arrival at Constantinople.

Constantinople : May 15, 1810.

P. S.—My dear H.,—The date of my postscript will 'prate to you of my whereabouts.' We anchored between the Seven Towers and the Seraglio on the 13th, and yesterday settled ashore. The ambassador is laid up ; but the secretary does the honours of the palace, and we have a general invitation to his table. In a short time he has his leave of audience, and we accompany him in our uniforms to the Sultan, &c., and in a few days I am to visit the Captain Pasha with the commander of our frigate. I have seen enough of their Pashas already ; but I wish to have a view of the Sultan, the last of the Ottoman race. Of Constantinople you have Gibbon's description, very correct as far as I have seen. The mosques I shall have a firman to visit. I shall most probably (Deo volente), after a full inspection of Stamboul, bend my course homewards; but this is uncertain. I have seen the most interesting parts, particularly Albania, where few Franks have ever been, and all the most celebrated ruins of Greece and Ionia. Of England I know nothing, hear nothing, and can find no person better informed on the subject than myself. I this moment drink your health in a bumper of hock; Hobhouse fills and empties to the same; do you and Drury pledge us in a pint of any liquid you please—vinegar will bear the nearest resemblance to that which I have just swallowed to your name; but when we meet again the draught shall be mended and the wine also.

Yours ever, B.

In a letter to Drury, written on the 17th of the next month, Byron writes:—

And Hodgson has been publishing more poesy. I wish he would send me his ' Sir Edgar ' and Bland's ' Anthology ' to Malta, whence they will be forwarded. . . . I wish you would write. I have heard from Hodgson frequently.

And on July 4, 1810, he writes from Constantinople as follows:—

My dear Hodgson,[1]—Twice have I written—once in answer to your last, and a former letter when I arrived here in May. That I may have nothing to reproach myself with, I will write once more—a very superfluous task, seeing that Hobhouse is bound for your parts full of talk and wonderment. My first letter went by an ambassadorial express; my second by the 'Black John' lugger; my third will be conveyed by Cam, the miscellanist. I shall begin by telling you, having only told it you twice before, that I swam from Sestos to Abydos. I do this that you may be impressed with proper respect for me, the performer; for I plume my-self on this achievement more than I could pos-sibly do on any kind of glory, political, poetical, or rhetorical. Having told you this I will tell you nothing more, because it would be cruel to curtail Cam's narrative, which, by-the-bye, you must not believe till confirmed by me, the eye-witness. I promise myself much pleasure from contradicting the greatest part of it. He has been plaguily pleased by the intelligence contained in your last to me respecting the reviews of his hymns. I re-freshed him with that paragraph immediately, together with the tidings of my own third edition,

---

[1] This letter has never been published.

which added to his recreation. But then he has had a letter from a Lincoln's Inn Bencher full of praise of his harpings, and vituperation of the other contributions to his *Missellingany,* which that sagacious person is pleased to say must have been put in as FOILS (horresco referens !) ; furthermore he adds that Cam 'is a genuine pupil of Dryden,' concluding with a comparison rather to the disadvantage of Pope. . . . I have written to Drury by Hobhouse ; a letter is also from me on its way to England intended for that matrimonial man. Before it is very long I hope we shall again be together ; the moment I set out for England you shall have intelligence, that we may meet as soon as possible. Next week the frigate sails with Adair ; I am for Greece, Hobhouse for England. A year together on the 2nd July since we sailed from Falmouth. I have known a hundred instances of men setting out in couples, but not one of a similar return. Aberdeen's party split ; several voyagers at present have done the same. I am confident that twelve months of any given individual is perfect ipecacuanha.

The Russians and Turks are at it, and the Sultan in person is soon to head the army. The Captain Pasha cuts off heads every day, and a

Frenchman's ears; the last is a serious affair. By-the-bye I like the Pashas in general. Ali Pasha called me his son, desired his compliments to my mother, and said he was sure I was a man of birth, because I had 'small ears and curling hair.' He is Pasha of Albania six hundred miles off, where I was in October—a fine portly person. His grandson Mahmout, a little fellow ten years old, with large black eyes as big as pigeon's eggs, and all the gravity of sixty, asked me what I did travelling so young without a Lala? (tutor).

Good night, dear H. I have crammed my paper and crave your indulgence. Write to me at Malta.

I am, with all sincerity, yours affectionately,

BYRON.

During an excursion in the Morea, which occupied the next few months, Lord Byron was attacked by a fever, which nearly proved fatal, at Patras near Missolonghi, where, fourteen years afterwards, he died of a similar complaint. On his partial recovery he wrote to Hodgson a letter dated Patras, Morea, Oct. 3, 1810, which is so illustrative of the intimacy then existing between them, and in many ways so characteristic of the writer, that its previous publication by Moore does not preclude the interest which the insertion of extracts from it here can hardly fail to excite.

As I have just escaped from a physician and a fever, which confined me five days to bed, you won't expect much 'allegrezza' in the ensuing letter. In this place there is an indigenous distemper, which, when the wind blows from the Gulf of Corinth (as it does five months out of six), attacks great and small, and makes woful work with visiters (sic). Here be also two physicians, one of whom trusts to his genius (never having studied) ; the other to a campaign of eighteen months against the sick of Otranto, which he made in his youth with great effect. When I was seized with my disorder, I protested against both these assassins; but what can a helpless, feverish, toast-and-watered poor wretch do? . . . In this state I made my epitaph —take it :—

> Youth, Nature, and relenting Jove,
> To keep my lamp in strongly strove ;
> But Romanelli was so stout,
> He beat all three—and blew it out.

But nature, being piqued at my doubts, did, in fact, beat Romanelli, and here I am well, but weakly, at your service.

Since I left Constantinople I have made a tour of the Morea, and visited Veley Pasha, who paid me great honours, and gave me a pretty stallion.

H. is doubtless in England before even the date of this letter: he bears a despatch from me to your bardship. . . . As for England, it is long since I have heard from it. Every one at all connected with my concerns is asleep, and you are my only correspondent, agents excepted. I have really no friends in the world; though all my old school companions are gone forth into that world, and walk about there in monstrous disguises, in the garb of guardsmen, lawyers, parsons, fine gentlemen, and such other masquerade dresses. So, I here shake hands and cut with all these busy people, none of whom write to me. Indeed I ask it not; and here I am, a poor traveller and heathenish philosopher, who hath perambulated the greatest part of the Levant, and seen a great deal of very improvable land and sea, and, after all, am no better than when I set out—Lord help me!

I have been out fifteen months this very day, and I believe my concerns will draw me to England very soon; but of this I will apprise you regularly from Malta. On all points Hobhouse will inform you, if you are curious as to our adventures. I have seen some old English papers up to the 15th of May. I see the 'Lady of the Lake' advertised. Of course it is in his old ballad style, and pretty.

After all, Scott is the best of them. The end of
all scribblement is to amuse, and he certainly suc-
ceeds there. I long to read his new romance.
And how does ' Sir Edgar ' and your friend Bland?

Dear H., remind Drury that I am his well-
wisher, and let Scrope Davies be well affected
towards me. I look forward to meeting you at
Newstead, and renewing our old champagne even-
ings with all the glee of anticipation. I have
written by every opportunity, and expect responses
as regular as those of the Liturgy, and somewhat
longer. As it is impossible for a man in his senses
to hope for happy days, let us at least look forward
to merry ones, which come nearest to the other in
appearance if not in reality ; and in such expectations I remain, &c.

Having returned to his head-quarters at Athens,
where he lived in the Franciscan Monastery, as afterwards at Venice with the Armenians, Byron wrote
again to his only English correspondent on November
14, 1810.

My dear Hodgson,[1]—This will arrive with an English
servant whom I send homewards with some papers

----

[1] This letter has not before been published.

of consequence. I have been journeying in different parts of Greece for these last four months,
and you may expect me in England somewhere
about April; but this is very dubious. Hobhouse
you have doubtless seen; he went home in August
to look after his Miscellany and to arrange materials
for a tour he talks of publishing. You will find
him well and scribbling; that is, scribbling if well,
and well if scribbling. I suppose you have a score
of new works, all of which I hope to see flourishing,
with a hecatomb of reviews. My works are likely
to have a powerful effect with a vengeance, as I
hear of divers angry people, whom it is proper I
should shoot at, by way of satisfaction. Be it so:
the same impulse which made 'Otho a warrior'
will make me one also. My domestic affairs being,
moreover, considerably deranged, my appetite for
travelling pretty well satiated with my late peregri-
nations, my various hopes in this world almost
extinct, and not very brilliant in the next, I trust I
shall go through the process with a creditable
'sang froid' and not disgrace a line of cut-throat
ancestors. I regret in one of your letters to hear
you talk of domestic embarrassments; indeed I am
at present very well calculated to sympathise with

you on that point. I suppose I must take to dram-drinking as a succedaneum for philosophy, though, as I am happily not married, I have very little occasion for either just yet. Talking of marriage puts me in mind of Drury (who, I suppose, has a dozen children by this time, all fine, fretful brats); I will never forgive matrimony for having spoiled such an excellent bachelor.

If anybody honours my name with an inquiry, tell them of 'my whereabouts,' and write if you like it. I am living alone in the Franciscan Monastery with one *Friar* (a Capucin of course) and one *Frier* (a bandy-legged Turkish cook), two Albanian savages, a Tartar, and a Dragoman : my only Englishman departs with this and other letters. The day before yesterday, the Waynode (or Governor of Athens) with the Mufti of Thebes (a sort of Mussulman Bishop) supped here with the Padre of the Convent, and my Attic feast went off with great eclât. I have had a present of a stallion from the Pasha of the Morea. I caught a fever going to Olympia. I was blown ashore on the Island of Salamis, in my way to Corinth through the Gulf of Ægina. I have kicked an Athenian postmaster, I have a friendship with the French Consul and an

Italian painter, and am on good terms with five
Teutones and Cimbri, Danes and Germans, who
are travelling for an academy. Vale!

Yours ever,

ΜΠΑΙΡΩΝ.

From the 'Volage' frigate, at sea, June 29, 1811,
Byron writes his last letter before reaching England,
in a strain of sadness half real and half assumed.

In a week, with a fair wind, we shall be at Ports-
mouth, and on the 2nd of July I shall have completed (to a day) two years of peregrination, from
which I am returning with as little emotion as I
set out. I think, upon the whole, I was more
grieved at leaving Greece than England, which I
am impatient to see, simply because I am tired of a
long voyage. Indeed, my prospects are not very
pleasant. Embarrassed in my private affairs,
indifferent to public, solitary without the wish to
be social, with a body a little enfeebled by a
succession of fevers, but a spirit, I trust, yet
unbroken, I am returning *home* without a hope,
and almost without a desire. The first thing I
shall have to encounter will be a lawyer ; the next
a creditor ; then colliers, farmers, surveyors, and all
the agreeable attachments to estates out of repair,

and contested coal-pits. In short, I am sick and sorry; and when I have a little repaired my irreparable affairs, away I shall march, either to campaign in Spain, or back again to the East, where I can at least have cloudless skies and a cessation from impertinence.

I trust to meet or see you, in town, or at Newstead, whenever you can make it convenient. I suppose you are in love and poetry as usual. That husband, H. Drury, has never written to me, albeit I have sent him more than one letter; but I daresay the poor man has a family, and of course all his cares are confined to his circle. I regretted very much in Greece having omitted to carry the 'Anthology' with me. What has 'Sir Edgar' done? And the 'Imitations and Translations;' where are they? I suppose you don't mean to let the public off so easily, but charge them home with a quarto. For me, I am sick of 'fops, and poesy, and prate,' and shall leave 'the whole Castalian state' to Bufo, or anybody else. But you are a sentimental and sensibilitous person, and will rhyme to the end of the chapter. Howbeit I have written some 4,000 lines, of one kind or another, on my travels. I need not repeat that I shall be happy to see you. I shall be in town about the

8th, at Dorant's Hotel in Albemarle Street, and
proceed in a few days to Notts, and thence to
Rochdale on business.

I am, here and there, yours, &c.

In his last letter from the 'Volage' frigate, off
Ushant, he writes to Drury, and at the end remarks :—

Hodgson, I suppose, is four deep by this time.
What would he have given to have seen, like me,
the *real Parnassus*, where I robbed the Bishop of
Chrissæ of a book of geography! But this I only
call plagiarism, as it was done within an hour's
ride of Delphi.

It was about this time that Hodgson wrote one of
those rhyming epistles to his friend, of which specimens have been already given.

> While modern Greeks, the shadows of their sires,
> Detain my Byron on that fabled shore,
> And cull faint murmurs from those sacred lyres
> That thrill'd the bosom of the world of yore ;
>
> Home-keeping still on England's happier plains,
> To native beauty sounds my faithful lay ;
> While native beauty smiles upon my strains,
> Why should I wish in Grecian woods to stray?

For genius high and cultured taste are here,
  And all that Athens in her pride could boast ;
The sage's eye that scans the glittering sphere,
  The patriot's ardour in itself a host.

Return then, Byron, to this favour'd land,
  For joy that flies thee cease in vain to roam ;
What joy can dwell with Turkey's slavish band?
  Thy own time-honour'd Newstead calls thee home.

Those mouldering walls where Phidias triumphs yet
  (If safe from Elgin's sacrilegious guile),
Can e'en their beauty bid thy soul forget
  Repentant Henry's consecrated pile?

Forget the scene, where loyal valour strove—
  Forget the ranks where godlike Falkland died—
Forget the youthful scene of promised love,
  Where love shall yet enjoy a fairer bride?

Return, my Byron ; to Britannia's fair,
  To that soft pow'r which shares the bliss it yields;
Return to Freedom's pure and vigorous air,
  To Love's own groves and Glory's native fields.

About three weeks after the last of these letters
was written the friends met in London ; but their first
meeting was interrupted by the arrival of other
visitors, and Hodgson gave expression to the warmth
of his feelings in the evening of the same day by the
following cordial effusion :—

My dear B.,—We were interrupted this morning in
our first interview ; I wish to prolong it, so con-
verse with me again.

> Alone, my Byron, at Harrovian springs—
> Yet not alone—thy joyous Hodgson sings ;
> The welcome image of his friend's return
> Fills his reviving heart, and bids it cease to mourn.
> O flow along, all unrestrain'd by art,
> Thou glad effusion of that grateful heart ;
> Tell his recover'd Byron, that once more
> It burns to see him on his native shore.
> It has not seen him yet !   For who can know,
> Disturb'd by common-place, that genuine glow
> Uninterrupted friendship sweetly feels,
> And wisdom from the world's vain commerce steals ?
> First let inspiring Health, and patriot Pride,
> Behold thee rank'd upon thy country's side ;
> First let thy country's foes severely feel
> Thy *caustic ardour* for the general weal.
> Spread, like a flame, my Byron, through the land
> That natural warmth no scoundrel can withstand ;
> That blaze of light, which folly's dearest shade
> Shall feel its inmost fastnesses invade.
> O'erthrow the bulwarks that corruption rears,
> And from proverbial dulness rescue half thy peers !
> Yet oh ! while Virtue fires let Prudence guide,
> Nor *argue*, when she hints, but then *decide*.
> Sage that advice immortal Horace gave,
> ' Oft laughing wit excels reflection grave ;'
> Nor less divine that second maxim flows,
> ' He writes the best who most correctly *knows*.'

He then shall *speak*, with Nature's noblest force,
Who, free from parliamentary remorse,
Untried, and pure, unpledged, and all his own,
By patient labour to full knowledge grown,
Shall weigh his country's power by sea, by land,
Shall half the foe's resources understand ;
Shall smoothe advice with reconciling wit,
And prove a Pericles but not a Pitt.
Athens ! my Byron ! Athens be thy aim !
Thy inspiration and thy guide to fame !
Not modern Athens—languid and impure,
Body and soul unworthy of a cure—
No, the fair land whose genius rose on high
Like yon Acropolis that mocks the sky ;
The sky where earlier suns more proudly shone,
On old Piræus, and old Marathon !

Adieu ! mon ami.

I am ever thine,

F. H.

That they met again after a few days is shown by a note written next day to Drury, in which Hodgson says :—

Byron prevented me from coming to you yesterday. He kept me so late in conversation, that I could get no farther than Kilburn in my walk, and then really thought it safer to return. He will come to you, if you can receive him, on Saturday next.

Send him word to Reddish's Hotel, St. James's Street. Griffiths has sent me a pressing letter for Don Roderick.

At the end of the month poor Byron, who had been reluctantly compelled to remain in town for the settlement of some legal and literary business, was suddenly summoned to Newstead by the serious illness of his mother, the news of whose death reached him on the road. Almost simultaneously with the announcement of this bereavement, he heard also of the deaths of his old Harrow schoolfellow Wingfield, and of one of his most cherished Cambridge colleagues, Charles Skinner Matthews, who was drowned while bathing in the Cam. Of this most melancholy catastrophe Drury wrote a graphic account immediately after its occurrence. Matthews was, as has been remarked, a young man of the greatest promise, and was a candidate for the representation of his University in Parliament at the ensuing election.

King's College, Cambridge.

My dear Hodgson,—All the way from Puckeridge to-day I was conning an extempore laughing epistle ; but have been so shocked with the account of poor Matthews's death, though I never saw him, that I can only write plain prose now. The reason I write is to request you not again to write to Hart on the subject. He *alone* saw him die—saw him in his very last agony—and but for him the body might have been at this moment beneath the waters. Not fifty of the strongest-bodied men in England could, without ropes, have given the slightest assistance. I am this moment returned with Hart from the spot. There is *literally* a bed of weeds, thick, more than *eight feet deep*. Poor Hart, I see, is sadly cut down.

These are the facts. You know the fork above the mills, thus—

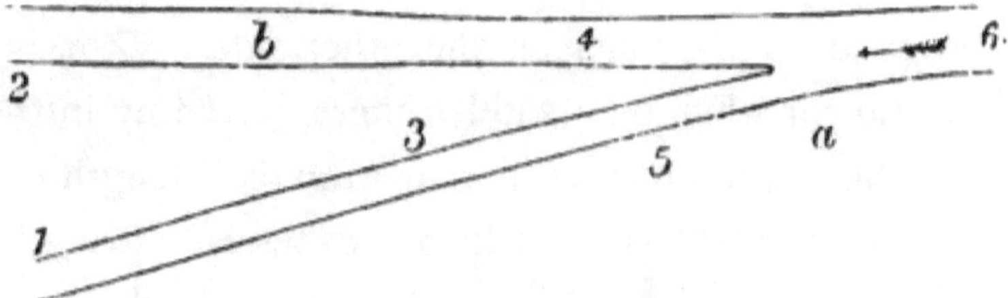

1. Newnham mills.
2. Queen's mills.
3. Spot where Hart was bathing.
4. Spot where Matthews was drowned.
5. Freshmen's pool.
6. Course of the river towards Grandchester.

Matthews had gone to bathe solo. Two gowns-men came, bathed, and left Freshmen's pool while he was bathing. From the best computation he

must have been in three-quarters of an hour.
These men (who did not know him) saw him (as in
bravado) stem down from points *a* and *b* what
seemed an inextricable mass of weeds; these he
cleared, had got down to *b*, and was returning—
the last they saw of him, as they went homewards.
Hart was alone on the bank when he distinctly
heard the cry of 'Help, help!' He had seen nobody in the water; but, directed by the noise, he
came to the spot. Nothing was to be seen. He
looked up and down the river (he was at a measured
140 yards off when the $\dot{\alpha}\rho\alpha\hat{\iota}\alpha$ $\phi\omega\nu\dot{\eta}$ first came to
him). He looked up and down the river some
time, as I said, and thought the person might have
escaped in the flags on the other side. Conceive
his horror when on a sudden there darted up in the
middle of the river a human form half-length out
of the water. He made an excessive struggle.
His arms were locked in weed; so were his legs and
thighs. You never saw such a place. He looked
most wistfully at Hart as if he knew him. Hart,
who had been incessantly holloaing ' Help!' (the two
men came back, but too late to see the last), called
to him, ' For Heaven's sake, Matthews, make no more
exertions; try to keep still till a rope is procured!'
In a resistless struggle Matthews then disentangled

the weeds from his arms (I saw the very weeds), and
threw them from him. This effort was his last ; as
if exhausted in it, he fell back. He was under the
water in an instant, and no trace was left of him.
Hart succeeded in having him got out in twelve
minutes ; but all too late. Every one who has
been on the spot highly commends all Hart did.
I verily think he nearly killed himself in his endeavours. The part of the river is the very
broadest. The weeds go from one bank to the other ;
and were, as I said, eight feet perpendicularly deep.
Temerity little short of madness could have induced
Matthews to attempt them. More when we meet.

God bless you, my dear friend !

HENRY DRURY.

Byron, as may well be imagined, was deeply
affected by these successive shocks ; and, becoming
impressed with the idea that he was himself destined to
die young, he made a will in which he bequeathed his

Household goods and furniture, library, pictures,
sabres, watches, plate, linen, trinkets, and other personal estate (except money and securities) to his
friends J. C. Hobhouse, S. B. Davies, and Francis
Hodgson, their executors, &c., to be equally divided
among them for their own use, requesting them to

accept the bequest therein contained to them respectively, as a token of his friendship.

On the 22nd of August he wrote a warm invitation to Newstead.

You will write to me? I am solitary, and I never felt solitude irksome before. Your anxiety about the critique on ——'s book is amusing; as it was anonymous, certes it was of little consequence. I wish it had produced a little more confusion, being a lover of literary malice. Are you doing nothing? writing nothing? printing nothing? Why not your ' Satire on Methodism? ' The subject (supposing the public to be blind to merit) would do wonders. Besides, it would be as well for a destined deacon to prove his orthodoxy. It really would give me pleasure to see you properly appreciated. I say *really*, as, being an author, my humanity might be suspected.

Believe me, dear H., yours always,

BYRON.

Four days later than the date of the above, the following pathetic verses were despatched to Hodgson. It is strange indeed that they should never have been previously published, as they must be admitted to be highly characteristic of their author, and vividly illustrative of that morbid melancholy which was now settling fast upon him.

Newstead Abbey : August 26, 1811.

I.

In the dome of my sires as the clear moonbeam falls
Through silence and shade o'er its desolate walls,
It shines from afar like the glories of old ;
It gilds, but it warms not—'tis dazzling, but cold.

II.

Let the sunbeam be bright for the younger of days :
'Tis the light that should shine on a race that decays,
When the stars are on high and the dews on the ground,
And the long shadow lingers the ruin around.

III.

And the step that o'erechoes the gray floor of stone
Falls sullenly now, for 'tis only my own ;
And sunk are the voices that sounded in mirth,
And empty the goblet, and dreary the hearth.

IV.

And vain was each effort to raise and recall
The brightness of old to illumine our hall ;
And vain was the hope to avert our decline,
And the fate of my fathers has faded to mine.

V.

And theirs was the wealth and the fulness of fame,
And mine to inherit too haughty a name ;
And theirs were the times and the triumphs of yore,
And mine to regret, but renew them no more.

VI.

And Ruin is fixed on my tower and my wall,
Too hoary to fade, and too massy to fall ;
It tells not of Time's or the tempest's decay,
But the wreck of the line that have held it in sway.

In answer to Drury's letter respecting the death of Matthews, Hodgson writes from the house of his uncle Mr. Coke, in Herefordshire, on September 1, 1811.

My dear Drury,—I send this to Walkerne, as I conclude you will have returned 'domum atque dulces liberos.' I have to thank you very much for your circumstantial letter concerning poor Matthews. It was unfortunate that I did not know Tom Hart was present at his death ; as I fear, by expressing what the wrong report in the newspapers suggested to many readers, I ignorantly offended him. I am truly sorry for the occasion, and trust he will as soon recover his spirits as can be expected after such an accident. He was sure to exert himself to the utmost.

Your 'Fen Gazette' also reached me and caused a hearty laugh. I ought to have acknowledged both these letters before. But our engagements in this country are most numerous. So much so, indeed, that I have been forced to neglect all my correspondents, and to write nothing for the Review. . . . Thank Mrs. D. for sending me your frank from Lord B. for the 28th of August and filling it up with such a delightful mélange.

How joyous is Bland's return! I have just heard from my cousin that he arrived (on the 20th I think) at Deal, in a licensed vessel, with a French passport. How he managed this I have yet to learn; but it is a most glorious escape. I hear he is looking uncommonly well, and is in very good spirits.

I have heard from Byron, who is at Newstead. The deaths of his mother and of his friend Matthews seemed to press heavily upon him. He tells me that a prosecution for a libel, published against him (in the 'Scourge'), is in the Attorney-General's hands, and will be brought forward in November. He begs me to come to Newstead—which I should much like to do—but I must first attend my mother to Bath or London, whichever she fixes upon. In October Byron talks of coming to Cambridge to see Davies [1]—of course I should rejoice to receive him there. You must tell me in your next your fen party. The good news about poor Hawtrey is delightful.

[1] Scrope Davies.

My best and kindest regards to Mrs. D.   The
bell tolls for breakfast, and another will soon toll for
church.   So adieu !

Ever yours,

F. H.

CHAPTER IX.

CORRESPONDENCE WITH BYRON ON RELIGIOUS SUBJECTS.

1811.

IT will have been observed that in the short poems addressed to Byron abroad, Hodgson more than once evinces anxiety on the score of his friend's religious difficulties. This anxiety was not likely to be lessened by the avowed infidelity expressed in the opening stanzas of the second canto of ' Childe Harold,' which Hodgson was now helping to correct for the press. The deep despondency into which the pilgrim had fallen since the rapid succession of deaths by which his return to Newstead had been saddened, seemed, moreover, to point to the abiding sorrow of one who mourned without hope.

Earnestly desirous of establishing sound religious principles in the mind of the young and ardent poet whose future was so full of bright promise for his country and for himself, while at the same time he offered such permanent consolation as can alone be afforded to the bereaved by the sure and certain hope in the resurrection to eternal life, Hodgson, who had already begun seriously to contemplate the obligations which ordination involves, wrote, with the affectionate zeal and well-timed consideration of true friendship, directing his friend's thoughts to the glorious inheritance which Christianity promises to its faithful adherents, in the prospect of a reunion with the departed in a blessed immortality.   Byron was widely but not deeply versed in philosophic and religious literature, and had been taught from boyhood, as has before been noticed, to identify Christianity with Calvinism. The point of view from which, about this period of his life, he regarded religious subjects may perhaps be best understood by the perusal of an unfinished letter to Gifford, written two years later, from which the following is a passage : 'I am no bigot to infidelity, and did not expect that, because I doubted the immortality of man, I should be charged with denying the existence of a God.   It was the comparative insignificance of ourselves and our world, when placed in comparison with the mighty whole of which it is an atom, that first led me to imagine that our pretensions to eternity might be overrated.   This, and

being early disgusted with a Calvinistic Scotch school
where I was cudgelled to church for the first ten years
of my life, afflicted me with this malady; for, after
all, it is, I believe, a disease of the mind, as much as
other kinds of hypochondria.'

This frank avowal proves that Hodgson's remon-
strances, which have unfortunately been lost, but to
which the following letters are answers, had, in all
probability, a far greater effect upon their recipient
than he cared, at the time, to admit; and that it was
their powerful, though perhaps unrecognised, influence
which induced him ever afterwards to speak in a far
more reverent tone of those great subjects, which,
whether a man believes, denies, or doubts, must be
admitted to be the most sacred of any which can
engage his thoughts.

In reading even these letters, deeply interesting
and instructive as they are, as throwing light upon
the history of such a mind, and as containing the
most explicit record extant of its religious sentiments,
if such they may be called, some allowance must
undoubtedly be made for the love of shocking prejudices, the fondness for making unprecedented statements and startling antitheses, which were so curiously
characteristic of their writer. Nor would it be fair to
ignore the distinction, which he himself elsewhere lays

down, between a sneering and desponding scepticism.
But, when these reservations and explanations have
been duly made, it is impossible to condemn too
severely the levity of several passages, or to deplore
too deeply the pervading spirit of defiant lawlessness
which degraded his mighty genius and noble, generous
nature to the lowest depths of a despairing doubt.

It will, moreover, be remarked that the observations are sometimes strangely superficial, and that the
arguments, though plausible enough, are illogical and
inconclusive ; and too often proceed upon that unsound system of à priori reasoning, which (as Hodgson
frequently observed of scepticism) limits the wisdom
of an omnipotent Creator by the ignorance of the imperfect creature.

Newstead Abbey : September 3, 1811.

My dear Hodgson,—I will have nothing to do with
your immortality ; we are miserable enough in this
life, without the absurdity of speculating upon
another.   If men are to live, why die at all? and if
they die, why disturb the sweet and sound sleep
that 'knows no waking'? 'Post mortem nihil est,
ipsaque mors nihil'—'quæris quo jaceas post
obitum loco?' 'Quo *non nata* jacent.' . . . As to
revealed religion, Christ came to save men ; but a

good Pagan will go to heaven, and a bad Nazarene to hell; 'Argal' (I argue like the gravedigger[1]) why are not all men Christians? or why are any? If mankind may be saved who never heard or dreamt, at Timbuctoo, Otaheite, Terra Incognita, &c., of Galilee and its Prophet, Christianity is of no avail; if they cannot be saved without, why are not all orthodox? It is a little hard to send a man preaching to Judæa, and leave the rest of the world— niggers and what not—dark as their complexions, without a ray of light for so many years to lead them on high; and who will believe that God will damn men for not knowing what they were never taught? I hope I am sincere; I was so at least on a bed of sickness in a far distant country, when I had neither friend, nor comforter, nor hope, to sustain me. I looked to death as a relief from pain, without a wish for an after-life, but a confidence that the God who punishes in this existence had left that last asylum for the weary.

$$\text{ὃν ὁ Θεὸς ἀγαπάει ἀπυθνήσκει νέος.}[2]$$

I am no Platonist, I am nothing at all; but I would sooner be a Paulician, Manichean, Spinozist,

---

[1] In *Hamlet*.   [2] He whom God loves dies young.

Gentile, Pyrrhonian, Zoroastian, than one of the seventy-two villanous sects who are tearing each other to pieces for the love of the Lord and hatred of each other. Talk of Galileeism? Show me the effects—are you better, wiser, kinder by your precepts? I will bring ten Mussulmen shall shame you all in good will towards men, prayer to God, and duty to their neighbours. And is there a ————,[1] or a Bonze, who is not superior to a fox-hunting curate? But I will say no more on this endless theme; let me live, well if possible, and die without pain. The rest is with God, who assuredly, had He *come* or *sent*, would have made Himself manifest to nations, and intelligible to all.

I shall rejoice to see you. My present intention is to accept Scrope Davies's invitation ; and then, if you accept mine, we shall meet *here* and *there*. Did you know poor Matthews? I shall miss him much at Cambridge.

The conclusion of this letter is unfortunately lost. Its first sentence seems to supply a most inadequate reason for rejecting the hope of immortality. If, as is implied, we are inevitably miserable in this life,

[1] The word here is illegible.

it is surely more consistent with God's justice and mercy—both of which appear to be admitted—that we should have further opportunities of attaining to happiness. To the alleged improbability that life should be renewed after death, it may be answered with confidence that such a process is not at variance, but quite in harmony, with the known method which the Almighty undoubtedly does adopt in His government of the universe. Purely poetical expressions and allusions to an obsolete system of Pagan ethics are hardly conclusive proofs to the contrary.

The fallacies contained in the succeeding statements are apparent enough. In the first place, it is unduly assumed that Christianity can never prevail among men; inasmuch as statistics plainly prove that from the date of its foundation its influences have been steadily, if slowly, increasing, and as there is every reason to believe that they will continue to increase until 'the earth shall be full of the knowledge of the Lord, as the waters cover the sea.' Secondly, that is emphatically asserted, which no reasonable person could seriously deny, that those to whom the Gospel message has never been offered cannot be considered responsible for its rejection.

What follows is so sadly and strangely prophetic, and so obviously devoid of all logical consistency, that its only possible answer is a sorrowful and sympathetic silence.

The scathing sarcasm of the next sentence was surely not much more or less justifiable sixty years ago than it is singularly appropriate to the contemptible disunions and controversies on non-essentials which characterise more modern Christianity ; but the unfairness of arguing generally against a creed because it necessarily involves abuses, is too manifest to demand serious comment. Of the conclusion it may be noticed that it certainly does not follow from the premisses ; but that, even if it did so follow, the premisses having been proved unsound, the conclusion would fall with them. The last words merely repeat the mistakes before pointed out, which ignore the doctrine of the gradual development of Christianity until to all is vouchsafed the opportunity of refusing the evil and of choosing the good.

The only answer from the recipient of these letters is the following fragment of verse, which may be taken as a clue to the spirit of the advice which elicited them :—

> Alone, my Byron, on Shelfordian plains,
> For thee I meditate my careless strains ;
> Roam, undisturb'd, in free-born thought along,
> And yield a day to friendship and to song.

Say, whence thy doubt of God's o'er-ruling pow'r,
Thou troubled dreamer of a darksome hour?
Is it that, dimly through this veil of sin,
The ray of virtue glimmers from within?
Is it that, soaring to sublimer things,
The flight of mind betrays her feeble wings?
But whence thy right, ephemeral phantom whence,
To purer instinct or to loftier sense?
Would Reason prompt thee louder to complain
If lower link'd in being's general chain?
She prompts not now thy discontented voice,
Nor bids thee choose where Heaven denies a choice.
What, if surrounded by a drearier shade,
Or by thy fate, or by thy folly made,
No beam of love illumed thy lonely path,
But, wandering on, an outcast child of wrath,
Without a guide, a father, or a friend,
Thy melancholy progress met its end,
Lost in the shoreless floods of silent space,
Thy time an instant, and a speck thy place.
What, if imprison'd in this ruin'd earth,
All traces gone of thy diviner birth,
Scarce could thy shuddering nature bear its doom,
The painful cradle, and the hopeless tomb!
What could'st thou more than blame thy Maker's
    plan,
And call His Providence the foe of man?
But praise Him now who gives unbounded scope
For Reason's honour, and for Virtue's hope;
Presents a world thy generous strength to try,
And spreads the prize of conquest in the sky.
What prize were that without an effort won?
Or why reward the deed that must be done?

No ! to thy choice is offer'd good or ill,
And conscience owns thy liberty of will.
Where then begin, where end, our fruitless strife?
Waive doubt awhile, and purify thy life.
Ask you what land contains the lustral fount?
Behold it flowing from Judæa's mount!
There weary pilgrims drink at Wisdom's shrine,
A water spotless from a source divine.
There pining cares and stormy passions rest,
And love dwells happy in the peaceful breast;
There Mercy weeps o'er human faults forgiven,
And Heav'n-born friendship reascends to Heav'n.
Say, can obedience lose the promised bliss?
Can Faith be groundless in a life like this?
No ! the cleansed heart assures the doubting eyes,
And new-born hopes to new-born virtues rise.
Then, ranging boundless o'er the Almighty whole
In every part a God ! shall strike the soul—
From one vast temple shall a God ! be heard;
A God from Judah's voice, a God ! from Nature's word.

.   .   .   .

As journeying darkly o'er the midnight heath,
The seeming reign of solitude and death,
Some fainting wretch pursues his fearful way;
Till o'er yon lengthening ocean gleams the day—
Wide and more wide the growing gold expands,
A cloudless glory lightens seas and lands!
Then lovely order through the prospect shines

.   .   .   .

The remainder of the verses is lost, but it is not
difficult to complete the simile.

If the wise counsels of this truest of friends had been allowed their legitimate force, and had exercised a more immediate influence upon the mind of the wayward poet, what a different future might, from that moment, have been opened to him! Untrammelled by the weaknesses of that lower nature which bound him down to earth, his mighty genius would have soared to loftier flights ; unfettered by the chains of a morbid self-consciousness, his noble, generous nature would have found scope for its energies in the exercise of the purest philanthropy. That marvellous combination of rank, and talent, and beauty, which made him alternately the idol and the scapegoat of his age, if tempered and guided by religious discipline, would have enabled him to confer incalculable benefits upon his fellow men. All that is grandest and noblest in human nature would henceforth have been inseparably associated with the name of Byron.

It is melancholy, indeed, to turn from the contemplation of such glorious possibilities to the strange reality of mingled faith and doubt which bore such bitter fruit ; lamentable, however deeply instructive, to look back upon the perilous rocks and subtly-shifting quicksands upon which so beautiful a bark was wrecked almost at the outset of its voyage.

Newstead Abbey : September 13, 1811.

My dear Hodgson,—I thank you for your song, or, rather, your two songs—your new song on love, and your *old song* on *religion*. I admire the *first* sincerely, and in turn call upon you to *admire* the following on Anacreon Moore's new operatic farce,[1] or farcical opera—call it which you will :—

> Good plays are scarce,
> So Moore writes farce ;
>   Is fame like his so brittle?
> We knew before
> That ' *Little's* ' *Moore*,
>   But now '*tis Moore* that's *Little*.

I won't dispute with you on the arcana of your new calling ; they are bagatelles, like the King of Poland's rosary. One remark, and I have done : the basis of your religion is *injustice* ; the *Son* of *God*, the *pure*, the *immaculate*, the *innocent*, is sacrificed for the *guilty*. This proves *His* heroism ; but no more does away *man's* guilt than a school-boy's volunteering to be flogged for another would exculpate the dunce from negligence, or preserve him from the rod. You degrade the Creator, in the first place, by making Him a begetter of

---

[1] The *M.P.*; *or, The Blue Stocking*, which, after having been acted for a few nights, disappeared finally from the stage.

children ; and in the next you convert Him into a tyrant over an immaculate and injured Being, who is sent into existence to suffer death for the benefit of some millions of scoundrels, who, after all, seem as likely to be damned as ever. As to miracles, I agree with Hume that it is more probable men should *lie* or be *deceived*, than that things out of the course of nature should so happen. Mahomet wrought miracles, Brothers the prophet had *proselytes*, and so would Breslau, the conjurer, had he lived in the time of Tiberius.

Besides, I trust that God is not a *Jew*, but the God of all mankind ; and, as you allow that a virtuous Gentile may be saved, you do away the necessity of being a Jew or a Christian.

I do not believe in any revealed religion, because no religion is revealed ; and if it pleases the Church to damn me for not allowing a *non-entity*, I throw myself on the mercy of the ' *Great First Cause, least understood*,' who must do what is most proper ; though I conceive He never made anything to be tortured in another life, whatever it may in this. I will neither read *pro* nor *con*. God would have made His will known without books, considering how very few could read them when Jesus of Nazareth lived, had it been His pleasure to ratify any peculiar mode of worship.   As to your immortality, if people are to live, why die ?   And our carcases, which are to rise again, are they worth raising ?   I hope, if mine is, that I shall have a better *pair of legs* than I have moved on these two-and-twenty years, or I shall be sadly behind in the squeeze into Paradise.   Did you ever read ' Malthus on Population ? '   If he be right, war and pestilence are our best friends, to save us from being eaten alive, in this ' best of all possible worlds.'

I will write, read, and think no more ; indeed, I do not wish to shock your prejudices by saying all I do think.   Let us make the most of life, and leave dreams to Emanuel Swedenborg.

Now to dreams of another genus—poesies.   I like your song much ; but I will say no more, for fear you should think I wanted to coax you into approbation of my past, present, or future acrostics. I shall not be at Cambridge before the middle of October ; but, when I go, I should certes like to see you there before you are dubbed a deacon.   Write to me, and I will rejoin.

Yours ever,

BYRON.

In this second letter, the first point to be noticed

is that the word 'injustice' is here used simply from a human point of view; and in discussing subjects which, from the very fact that they are still subjects of discussion, are proved to be beyond the comprehension of man's finite intelligence, it is important that we lose not sight of the evident probability that God has fuller, wider notions of justice than man, by the circumstances of his constitution, can possibly entertain; that His judgments are inscrutable, and His ways past finding out. Again, the voluntary character of the sacrifice of Him, who took upon Him our nature, is virtually ignored; while the tangible and visible effects of Christianity throughout the world are also completely set aside or forgotten.

The great subject of miracles is dismissed in so summary a manner as to render a distinct refutation of the opinion definitely expressed impossible, without an exhaustive inquiry into the credibility of witnesses such as is to be found in Paley's 'Evidences;' or a comprehensive consideration of the whole subject of God's omnipotence, and consequent power to change for a specific and unique purpose the laws which He has made, such as is amply afforded by Butler's 'Analogy.'

To the truism that God is the God of all mankind, it may be answered that the doctrines of Christianity are in no way really antagonistic to such a notion ; but that, as was noticed in answer to a similar statement in the former letter, only those are condemned who persistently reject a religion which not only promises present and future happiness, but which is proved by constant experience to have a power to guide and assist its faithful adherents to happy and honourable lives, and to assure them of calm and peaceful deaths. In the next place, when it is asserted that no religion is *revealed*, it is necessary to inquire what is the exact sense in which the word is used, and to bear in mind the fact that the natural processes, the results of which we daily see and feel, are certainly not clearly revealed to us ; that *revelation*, however applied, is a relative term, and involves questions of degree. For that the world in which we live and move and have our being is full of hidden mysteries, will hardly be denied even by those who are most sceptical on the subject of revealed religion. And the positive fact that prayer is constantly answered is not more miraculous or less mysterious than many of the natural events by which we are surrounded, but for which we cannot fully account. Nor is it more consistent with the idea of God's merciful justice to suppose that He would allow His creatures to be deceived into the false belief that they will be punished hereafter, than to imagine Him determined to punish hereafter those who resolutely resist His will, and often go unpunished here. But the words which follow may fairly be considered to contain the clue to much which precedes them. 'I will read neither *pro* nor *con*.' Does not this plainly point to the predetermined resolve of one whose wish was father to his thought, and who preferred to make his principles tally with his practice, rather than to adopt such religious tenets as would inevitably lead to the necessity of an unwelcome discipline of life.

That God did make His will known without books, as well as through them, is proved by the unprecedented and unparalleled effects of the Apostles' teaching, and to the widespread influences of oral instructions and traditions throughout the early ages of the Church's history.

The painfully irreverent allusion to the doctrine of the resurrection of the body is an instance of the determination (so characteristic of its writer) to press forcibly to their natural conclusion any opinions which arrested his attention. But it is strange that he should have altogether overlooked the Christian belief that the natural body which dies is raised a spiritual body ; that there are bodies terrestrial and bodies celestial.

In these days of universal inquiry and rigid criticism, the consideration of the religious sentiments of so powerful a thinker as Byron, if conducted in a conscientious spirit, cannot be devoid of useful interest. For the necessary conviction which such a consideration will inculcate is obviously this : that if *such a mind* could find no stronger arguments than these in favour of scepticism, Christianity, however it might suffer temporarily from the insensibility of its opponents, would be in no danger of ultimate suppression even if it depended solely upon human agencies for its support ; while the fatal influences of such self-reliant speculations are strikingly exemplified in the hapless life and premature death of the greatest poet of his age.

CHAPTER X.

LETTERS FROM BYRON—MEETING AT CAMBRIDGE
—PREVENTION BY HODGSON OF DUEL BETWEEN
BYRON AND MOORE—VISIT TO NEWSTEAD—
MORE LETTERS.

1811–12.

A WEEK after the last of the letters in the last
chapter was written, Byron writes to Dallas: 'I have
brought you and my friend Juvenal Hodgson on my
back, on the score of revelation. You are fervent, but
he is quite glowing. I honour and thank you both
but am convinced by neither,' &c.; and four days
later to Hodgson himself.

Newstead Abbey: September 25, 1811.

My dear Hodgson,—I fear that before the latest of
October or the first of November, I shall hardly
be able to make Cambridge. My everlasting agent
puts off his coming like the accomplishment of a
prophecy. However, finding me growing serious
he hath promised to be here on Thursday, and

VOL. I.   P

about Monday we shall remove to Rochdale. I have only to give discharges to the tenantry here (it seems the poor creatures must be raised, though I wish it was not necessary) and arrange the receipt of sums, and the liquidation of some debts, and I shall be ready to enter upon new subjects of vexation. I intend to visit you in Granta, and hope to prevail on you to accompany me here or there or anywhere.

My tortoises (all Athenians), my hedgehog, my mastiff, are all purely. The tortoises lay eggs, and I have hired a hen to hatch them. I am writing notes for *my* quarto[1] (Murray would have it a *quarto*), and Hobhouse is writing text for *his* quarto; if you call on Murray or Cawthorn you will hear news of either. I have attacked De Pauw, Thornton, Lord Elgin, Spain, Portugal, the 'Edinburgh Review,' travellers, painters, antiquarians and others, so you see what a dish of sour crout controversy I shall prepare for myself. It would not answer for me to give way, now; as I was forced into bitterness at the beginning, I will go through to the last. 'Væ Victis.' If I fall, I shall fall gloriously, fighting against a host.

Felicissima Notte a Voss. Signoria.

B.

---

[1] *Childe Harold.*

Hodgson, deeply distressed at the tone of these last letters—a tone which he knew to be partly real and partly assumed, and earnestly desirous that his friend should share the happiness which his own kindly and contented disposition enabled him to enjoy—wrote some verses in a cheerful and joyous strain, exhorting Byron to look at the brighter side of life, and to banish care. Byron immediately responded in those eminently characteristic and now celebrated lines [1] in which he alludes to his early disappointment in love as the source of all his subsequent sorrow. When in 1829 Hodgson sent these verses to Moore, for insertion in the 'Life,' which was then being compiled, he carefully drew his pen through the concluding lines, and wrote below them, 'From hence to the end to be left out as agreed with Moore. F. H.' This stipulation, however, Moore, as in many other cases, entirely disregarded. The lines marked for omission are these :—

> But if, in some succeeding year,
> When Britain's 'May is in the sere,'
> Thou hear'st of one whose deepening crimes
> Suit with the sablest of the times ;
> Of one, whom love nor pity sways,
> Nor hope of fame, nor good men's praise ;

[1] *Epistle to a Friend.*

> One, who in stern ambition's pride,
> Perchance not blood shall turn aside ;
> One rank'd in some recording page
> With the worst anarchs of the age ;
> Him wilt thou *know*, and, *knowing*, pause,
> Nor with the *effect* forget the *cause*.

In the margin of the original copy Hodgson writes :
—' N.B. The poor dear soul meant nothing of this.
F. H.'

This note speaks volumes ; coming as it does
from one who knew the poet so intimately, and who
understood the strangely blended contrasts of his
character perhaps better than any other one of his
friends.   It has often been remarked that Byron
loved to identify himself with ' the dark sublime he
drew.'   There can be no stronger confirmation of the
fact than these few words, which go far to dispel the
many misunderstandings and illusions by which his
great name has so long been surrounded.

Two days later he sent a long letter to Hodgson,
published by Moore, in which he writes : ' I don't
know that I shan't end with insanity, for I want a
method in arranging my thoughts that perplexes me
strangely ; but this looks more like silliness than
madness, as Scrope Davies would facetiously remark
in his consoling manner.   I must try the hartshorn of
your company.'   And again at the end : ' Write and

send me your " Love Song "—but I want *paulò majora*
from you. Make a dash before you are a deacon,
and try a *dry* publisher. Yours always,   B.'

The dry allusion is to Mr. Payne, of the firm of
Payne & Mackinlay, who had published Hodgson's
' Juvenal.' Payne had lately committed suicide by
drowning himself in the Paddington Canal.

It was at the end of this month (October) that
Byron paid his promised visit to Cambridge, where
many matters, religious and poetical, were doubtless
discussed in detail by the friends. During this visit a
letter from Moore (the first which Byron ever received
from him) was forwarded from Newstead, calling his
attention to a former letter written from Dublin
on January 1, 1810, in which an explanation was
required of certain expressions used by Byron in
' English Bards,' with reference to Moore's ' leadless '
and therefore bloodless duel with Jeffrey at Chalk
Farm ; and, failing such explanation, satisfaction was
demanded.

This former letter, having been despatched soon
after Lord Byron's departure from England, was
placed by the friend to whom Moore had entrusted it,
in Hodgson's hands. Having been made aware, by
the manner of its delivery, of the nature of this letter,
and feeling sure that his friend's impetuous and fiery

disposition would at once lead him to consider that it constituted a direct challenge to fight a duel, Hodgson, on his own responsibility, determined to suppress it until the feeling of irritation which occasioned it should have been obliterated by time. But this second letter of Moore's placed him in an apparently inextricable dilemma. For he had already, as in duty bound, reminded Byron in London on his return, that he had such a letter in his possession ; of which Byron's sudden summons to Newstead had enabled him still further to postpone the delivery. Now they were together again and Moore repeated his complaints, though in a somewhat modified form, and requested a further explanation of the delay which had occurred in the reply to his first letter. Still Hodgson somehow contrived to keep it back until continued correspondence with Moore turned enmity into friendship ; its delivery became unnecessary ; and it was returned *in statu quo* to the writer, at his own suggestion. Thus England was spared the spectacle of a duel between Moore and Byron. Thus a catastrophe was averted which might have resulted fatally to one or both of two of the greatest poets of their time ; a disaster by which the world of literature would have been robbed of some of its most priceless treasures. It is impossible to overestimate the consummate tact

and firmness displayed by Hodgson in this most difficult and delicate episode of peacemaking diplomacy.

Moore's letter was written on the 30th October.
A fortnight later Byron wrote from London to Hodgson at Cambridge, laconically, but in a very large
hand underlined, 'Send a certain letter. B.' ; and
after two days, having received no answer, he wrote
again :—

8 St. James's Street : November 17, 1811.

Dear Hodgson,—I have been waiting for the *letter*,
which was to be sent by you *immediately*, and
must again jog your memory on the subject. I
have heard from Hobhouse, who has at last sent
more copy to Cawthorn for his 'Travels.' I franked
an enormous cover for you yesterday, seemingly to
convey at least twelve cantos on any given subject.
I fear the aspect of it was too *epic* for the post.
From this and other coincidences I augur a publication on your part, but what or when, or how
much, you must disclose immediately.

I don't know what to say about coming down
to Cambridge at present, but live in hopes. I am
so completely superannuated there, and besides
feel it something brazen in me to wear my magis-
terial habit, after all my buffooneries, that I hardly
think I shall venture again. And being now an

'ἄριστον μὲν ὕδωρ' disciple I won't come within wine-
shot of such determined topers as your collegiates.
I have not yet subscribed to Bowen. I mean to
cut Harrow '*enim unquam*' as somebody classically
said for a farewell sentence. I am superannuated
there too, and, in short, as old at twenty-three as
many men at seventy.

Do write and send this letter that hath been so
long in your custody. It is of importance that M.
should be certain I never received it, if it be *his*.
Are you drowned that I have never heard from
you, or are you fallen into a fit of perplexity?
Cawthorn has declined, and the MS. is returned to
him. This is all at present from yours in the faith,

ΜΠΑΙΡΩΝ.

The conclusion of the next letter proves that
Hodgson's considerate counsel on religious subjects
had, at all events, greater influence with its recipient
than he was at present prepared to admit. The
words 'I deny nothing' point to an altered frame of
mind ; and universal doubt, however unsatisfactory, is
a decided improvement upon absolute unbelief.

8 St. James's Street : December 4, 1811.

My dear Hodgson,—I have seen Miller, who will see
Bland, but I have no great hopes of his obtaining

the translation [1] from the crowd of candidates.
Yesterday I wrote to Harness, who will probably
tell you what I said on the subject. Hobhouse
has sent me my Romaic MSS., and I shall require
your aid in correcting the press, as your Greek eye
is more correct than mine. But these will not
come to type this month, I dare say. I have put
some soft lines on ye Scotch in the 'Curse of
Minerva,' take them :

> Yet Caledonia claims some native worth, &c.

If you are not content now, I must say with the
Irish drummer to the deserter who called out,
'Flog high, flog low'—'The de'il burn ye, there's
no pleasing you, flog where one will.'

I have read Watson to Gibbon. He proves
nothing, so I am where I was, verging towards
Spinoza ; and yet it is a gloomy creed, and I want
a better, but there is something pagan in me that I
cannot shake off. In short, I *deny nothing*, but
doubt everything. The post brings me to a conclusion. Bland has just been here.

Yours ever,
BN.

[1] The translation of *Charlemagne*, an epic poem by Prince Lucien
Bonaparte, afterwards undertaken by Francis Hodgson conjointly with
Samuel Butler, Head-master of Shrewsbury, and subsequently Bishop
of Lichfield.

In the next letter, dated London, December 8, 1811, and partly published by Moore, Byron writes :—

I sent you a sad 'Tale of Three Friars' the other day, and now take a dose in another style.   I wrote it a day or two ago, on hearing a song of former days :—

Away, away, ye notes of woe, etc.

I have gotten a book by Sir W. Drummond (printed but not published) entitled 'Œdipus Judaicus,' in which he attempts to prove the greater part of the Old Testament an allegory, particularly Genesis and Joshua.   He professes himself a theist in the preface, and handles the literal interpretation very roughly.   I wish you could see it.   Mr. Ward has lent it to me, and I confess to me it is worth fifty Watsons.   You and Harness must fix on the time for your visit to Newstead. . . .   Master William Harness and I have recommenced a most fiery correspondence ;   I like him as Euripides liked Agatho, or Darby admired Joan, as much for the past as the present.

In the postscript of the next letter he adds : ' I only wait for your answer to fix our meeting.'   A few days later this meeting took place at Newstead, between Byron, Harness, and Hodgson.   Moore, who had also been invited, was unable to come.   Harness left a most interesting sketch [1] of his visit, in which the allusions to Hodgson are so pointed that they can hardly be omitted from a memoir of his life.

When Byron returned, with the MS. of the first two cantos of 'Childe Harold' in his portmanteau, I paid him a visit at Newstead.[2]   It was winter— dark, dreary weather—the snow upon the ground ; and a straggling, gloomy, depressive, partially- inhabited place the Abbey was.   Those rooms, however, which had been fitted up for residence were so comfortably appointed, glowing with crim- son hangings, and cheerful with capacious fires, that one soon lost the melancholy feeling of being domiciled in the wing of an extensive ruin.   Many tales are related or fabled of the orgies which, in the poet's early youth, had made clamorous these ancient halls of the Byrons.   I can only say that nothing in the shape of riot or excess occurred when I was there.   The only other visitor was Dr. Hodgson,[3] the translator of 'Juvenal,' and

[1] Quoted by Mr. L'Estrange in his *Literary Life of the Rev. Wm. Harness.*

[2] It will be observed that this visit took place several months after Byron's return.

[3] This is a mistake.   Hodgson, at this time, was not even ordained, and never took the Doctor's degree, even when Provost of Eton.

nothing could be more quiet and regular than the
course of our days. Byron was retouching, as the
sheets passed through the press, the stanzas of
'Childe Harold.' Hodgson was at work in getting
out the ensuing number of the 'Monthly Review,'
of which he was principal editor. I was reading
for my degree. When we met, our general talk
was of poets and poetry—of who could or who
could not write; but it occasionally rose into very
serious discussions on religion. Byron, from his
early education in Scotland, had been taught to
identify the principles of Christianity with the
extreme dogmas of Calvinism. His mind had
thus imbibed a most miserable prejudice, which
appeared to be the only [1] obstacle to his hearty
acceptance of the Gospel. Of this error we were
most anxious to disabuse him. The chief weight
of the argument rested with Hodgson, who was
older, a good deal, than myself. I cannot even
now—at a distance of more than fifty years—recall
those conversations without a deep feeling of
admiration for the judicious zeal and affectionate
earnestness (often speaking with tears in his eyes)
which Dr. Hodgson evinced in his advocacy of the

---

[1] It will be seen from the foregoing letters that this is hardly a complete statement of the case.

truth. The only difference, except perhaps in the subjects talked about, between our life at Newstead Abbey and that of the great families around us, was the hours we kept. It was, as I have said, winter, and the days were cold ; and, as nothing tempted us to rise early, we got up late. This flung the routine of the day rather backward, and we did not go early to bed. My visit to Newstead lasted about three weeks, when I returned to Cambridge to take my degree.

About the middle of the next month, January 1812, Hodgson also returned to Cambridge, and Byron went to London to his old quarters in St. James's Street. Several letters passed between them, but not upon subjects of public interest. Byron was again possessed by a feeling of the deepest melancholy, and seems to have recurred to his old sorrow, the early disappointment in love, which he appears to have attributed partly to that slight physical infirmity on which he often dwelt so painfully. He writes to Hodgson with reference to another object of affection : 'I do not blame her, but my own vanity in fancying that such a thing as I am could ever be beloved.' He also recurred to the numerous deaths of friends which had rendered his return to England so melancholy, and especially that of Eddlestone, and wrote : 'There is one consolation in Death—where he sets his seal the impression can neither be melted nor broken, but endureth for ever. I almost rejoice when one I love dies young, for I could never bear to see them old or altered.' He was, moreover, harassed with business and lawyers, whom he describes as being in a 'pestilent hurry all about affidavits.' Hodgson again endeavoured to cheer him, and to divert his thoughts into a different channel by inducing him to exert his powers in Parliament. This advice was not disregarded, an ambition of oratorical distinction was aroused, and efforts were made towards its attainment by careful preparation. The first intimation of the existence of this new interest occurs in a letter to Hodgson dated 8 St. James's Street, February 1, 1812 :—

I am rather unwell with a vile cold, caught in the House of Lords last night. Lord Sligo and myself, being tired, *paired off*, being of opposite sides, so that nothing was gained or lost by *our* votes. I did not speak ; but I might as well, for nothing could have been inferior to (those who did). The Catholic Question comes on this month, and perhaps I may then commence. I must 'screw my courage to the sticking place, and we'll *not* fail.'

Yours ever,

B.

While the preparation for the great speech on the Frame-breaking Bill was going on, and with 'Childe Harold' in the press, Byron yet found time for the following humorous and good-natured appeal in behalf of a friend and aspiring author :—

London : February 21, 1812.

My dear Hodgson,—There is a book entituled ' *Galt, his Travels in ye Archipelago,*' daintily printed by Cadell and Davies, ye which I could desiderate might be criticised by you, inasmuch as ye author is a well-respected esquire of mine acquaintance, but I fear will meet with little mercy as a writer, unless a friend passeth judgment. Truth to say, ye boke is ye boke of a cock-brained man, and is full of devices crude and conceitede, but peradventure for my sake this grace may be vouchsafed unto him. Review him myself I can not, will not, and if you are likewize hard of heart, woe unto ye boke, ye which is a comely quarto.

Now then ! I have no objection to review if it

pleases Griffiths to send books, or rather *you*, for you know the sort of things I like to play with. You will find what I say very serious as to my intentions. I have every reason to induce me to return to Ionia. Believe me,

Yours always,
B.

The earliest, and indeed the only original, account of his first and most famous speech, was sent to Hodgson, and is published by Moore, with the exception of this sentence, '*I hire myself unto Griffiths, and* my poesy comes out on Saturday.' Griffiths was the editor of the 'Monthly,' but there is no record of any contribution to it from Byron, and he afterwards refused to review at all.

The poesy thus unostentatiously mentioned was the immortal 'Childe Harold;' and immediately after its publication, Byron, who, as he concisely puts it, 'woke up one morning and found himself famous,' now plunged into the vortex of London society, which at once paid him that unprecedented homage, amounting almost to idolatry, which was sustained for a time through the combined influences of his rank and genius, as well as by the irresistible charms of his manner and appearance. Hodgson remained quietly at Cambridge, lecturing, reviewing, and maintaining a constant correspondence with his numerous friends. He occasionally went to London, and never without visiting and conversing with Lord Byron.

CHAPTER XI.

ORIGIN OF BLAND'S 'ANTHOLOGY'—HODGSON'S CON-
TRIBUTIONS TO IT—SKETCH OF BLAND'S LIFE
AND PASSAGES FROM HIS LETTERS.

1812.

THE ' Anthology,' to which Hodgson made considerable contributions, was republished in a revised form
in the year 1812.   This celebrated work first appeared
in 1806, Bland and Merivale being its principal
editors, and was soon greeted with the admiration
which it so fully deserved. Byron, in one of his
letters to Hodgson, says that he ' always bewailed its
absence' during his Grecian travels, and in his Satire
he thus apostrophises its authors :—

> And you associate bards ! who snatch'd to light
> Those gems too long withheld from modern sight ;
> Whose mingling taste combined to cull the wreath,
> Where Attic flowers Aonian odours breathe,
> And all their renovated fragrance flung
> To grace the beauties of your native tongue.

Some years after Bland's death a proposal was made

by some of his friends to write a memoir of his life, and Merivale then gave the following account of the origin of their joint work :—

I can hardly say that my acquaintance with Bland commenced so early as during our residence at college, but I was accidentally thrown into his company two or three times in the course of that period ; once, in particular, I well remember, in a walking party to Wimpole, the seat of Lord Hardwicke, consisting, besides himself and myself, of Harry Drury, Twiss (now Dr. Twiss), the present Lord Chancellor (then Charles Pepys), and I forget who else. I remember little respecting it except that we were all very light-hearted and merry, and poor Bland conspicuous for that peculiar species of whim and extravaganza which procured for him in after times, among the *dramatis personæ* of a proposed burletta by our friend (now Archdeacon) Hodgson on the model of Fielding's Covent Garden tragedy, the appropriate designation of ' Don Hyperbolo.' But our intimacy must be referred for its commencement to the time when, after leaving college, he became settled as an assistant-master at Harrow, where I was a frequent visitor, and when (principally under Harry Drury's auspices) a social club, or circle, was early formed, of which, besides us three, Denman (now Lord Chief Justice), Hodgson (now Archdeacon of Derby), Walford (solicitor to the Customs), Paley (son of Archdeacon Paley, and a brother collegian of Bland at Pembroke—long since, alas! taken from us), Pepys, and Shadwell[1], and a few more, less closely united with us in youthful sport and frolic, may be enumerated as members. In the compass of a very few years marriage and the consequent accession of domestic and professional cares and pursuits, in a great degree operated as the dissolution of our society, but not of our mutual regard and friendship. Several bonds of union still subsisted among us, and, with regard to some at least of our fraternity, a similarity of taste in literature and poetry constituted by no means the weakest of them.

It so happened that both Bland and myself, while at college, though then unknown to each other, had committed divers sins of the poetical sort in attempted translations from the Greek minor poets and epigrammatists. When our friendship commenced at Harrow, we soon compared notes—thence proceeded to mutual exten-

[1] Launcelot Shadwell, Vice-Chancellor.

sion of our collections—and finally decided to launch on the perilous undertaking of joint author- ship, under the liberal patronage of that great Mæcenas of literature, Richard Phillips (now Sir Richard), publisher of the 'Monthly Magazine.' It was, accordingly, in that very respectable miscel- lany that we started on our career as 'brother bards,' on the 1st of March, 1805, in a paper headed with the title 'Epigrams, Fragments, and Fugitive Pieces from the Greek,' to which was subjoined the signature 'Narva,' an appellative borrowed (as I well remember) from a poem of Chatterton's, which, *euphoniæ gratiâ*, for I think it possessed no other merit, was just then constantly in the mouth of our friend Hodgson, who graciously permitted the name to be transferred to ourselves. This first and the three or four succeeding numbers comprised the greater part of the materials from which Bland composed the preface to our subsequent volume, published in 1806, entitled 'Translations, chiefly from the Greek Anthology, with Tales and Miscel- laneous Poems'; and it was not long before our youthful senses were regaled with the tribute of praise from unknown writers.

About this time Denman wrote to Hodgson *à propos* of the 'Anthology':—

I am infinitely too much flattered by your request to hesitate a moment about complying
with it, though I sincerely think the compositions will add no value to your publication,
and would do no credit to their author, if
he was known. I will beg, therefore, that you
will not mention his name to any but those who
already know it. The trouble of revising will, I fear,
be greater than you seem to anticipate ; but most
especially I desire that if your opinion of them
should change on a subsequent perusal, you will
not think it necessary to print them, in consequence
of your present application. Most sincerely do I
hope that you will keep your promise of being with
us more frequently when you are in town.

Two of the poems thus modestly referrèd to by
their author were two translations of the Ode on
the Athenian Patriots, Harmodius and Aristogiton,
by Callistratus (Scol. 7, 1, 155). The version beginning with the words 'In myrtle my sword will
I wreathe,' is mentioned by Byron in a note[1] to
'Childe Harold,' as the best English translation.

Two very beautiful fragments by Hodgson, on a
pipe in the Temple of Venus, and on a laurel beside

[1] Canto iii. stanza 20.

a fountain, are translated into Latin elegiacs by Dr. Kennedy in the 'Sabrinæ Corolla.'

It is strange that so exquisite a collection of classical gems as the 'Anthology' should have been so long allowed to remain out of print.

Of its talented but eccentric editor, Robert Bland, the surviving notices are scanty. He was appointed to a chaplaincy at Amsterdam, whence he returned to his native land in 1811, after having travelled in disguise through a considerable part of the Continent, during the most perilous period of the French supremacy. On his return he obtained, through the influence of his friends, a desirable curacy at Kenilworth, where he eked out a slender income by the precarious occupation of taking pupils, and died from breaking a blood-vessel in 1825, at the early age of 45. Besides the 'Anthology' he published several original poems, the best of which were 'Edwy and Elgiva,' and the 'Four Slaves of Cythera.'

Some extracts from his correspondence are not without interest, both from the date at which they were written, and for the humorous extravagances with which they abound. They are addressed to Merivale, and the first is dated August 9, 1805, St. Alban's Street,[1] Wednesday, *midnight.*

[1] The residence of his father, Dr. Bland, the eminent physician.

Many and the most sincere thanks for your very kind
letter. I really am obliged to you for being so
happy as you mention, although I think you might
have been so without endeavouring to make me
envious. And so you wish me to follow your
example.[1]   If any person would accommodate me
with the trifling sum of a cool £10,000, I would
really do so. But if you only reflect on the treasures contained in my table drawer, you might find
1,000 pounds worth of reasons for remaining as I
am—stupid, flat, dull and solitary. . . . You
will excuse the gloom of this letter, when you consider the solemn hour at which I write, and the
more so as you know that I seldom, if ever, write
to entertain others, but only when I am a burthen
to myself, and wish to lay part of the load on some
one else. But, what is the best excuse of all, I have
this evening returned to London from ———, where
I have been leading the life of a god for these five
days. On Friday ———'s birthday, concert, fire
and water works, ball, supper; so that Friday was certainly not so bad ; though, to my mind, all the squibs
and crackers and rockets and what-d'ye-call-'ems,
produced by gunpowder, together with set concerts,
suppers, balls, and nicknackeries, are not worth this

[1] Merivale had lately married.

pinch of snuff. No, sir. It was Saturday, passed on the lawn, with a soft, sick, languid, and amiable headache, charmed away by a late breakfast and vocal music (particularly by hearing myself sing),[1] dance on the green, dinner, music, dance again, singing again till two in the morning, and all in a private family party—it was this, continued for three or four days, that did the business, and made me what I am—gloomy, and discontented. Mrs. ——— recited several beautiful scraps of poems ; I retaliated with your 'Clarissa,' your 'O'er the Smooth Main,' and Hodgson's 'Moderate Wishes.' The sensation was so great, that, drunk as I was with pleasure at hearing my friends applauded, I was on the verge of reciting something of my own and should have done so—but (luckily) I forgot everything, and so was saved the disgrace of being hissed off the stage. The lines of my own which I was near venturing, were the description of the wood, and hags that haunted it, in 'Edwy and Elgiva,' which are the best lines I have written. Very luckily I forgot the second verse, and consequently could not begin the first with any propriety. There is a charm, my dear Merry, in that house, which sets a man at ease in a moment. No vul-

---

[1] All his contemporaries agreed in admiring his singing.

garity, no quizzing, but the most elegant persons
with the most elegant manners—music the most
celestial, and, as one cannot get higher than celestial, manners the most engaging. Had the whole
business of their lives been to please, and they had
studied their profession from their births, they
could not have succeeded better.   And here I must
not omit mentioning that flattery is one source of
pleasure. None of your stiff, awkward compliments
that break the teeth of the speaker, and make the
hearer look like a fool ; but kind, good-natured
hints of approbation, that encourage people to talk,
to amuse and be amused.   I really cannot fix my
eye upon any five days that have been so varied
with all manner of delights.   I would change the
subject which, however interesting to myself, can
have no great share of interest to you, only, as *you*
talked of nothing but *yourself* (and I like you for
it), do let me talk of ————.   Then we dined in a
wood—pretty thought !—' our seat the turf, our
canopy the sky.' All the oreads, dryads, and naiads
were delighted with our music.   ' Satyrs and sylvan
boys were seen, peeping from out their alleys
green.'   The evening passed in reading, recitation,
music, supping (*pro formâ*—that is to say, as an
excuse for assembling round a table, rather than

for the sake of gross eating and drinking). After
singing and all the etceteras, we went to our repose,
each highly satisfied with the day, and with the
quota of entertainment that each had contributed.
The poet sought his pillow, delighted and perfectly
satisfied with his own bad verses ; the rebus, riddle,
and conundrum-makers with their subtleties; the
explainers of the same with their acuteness; the
vocal performers with their voices; the instrumental
with their fingers; and, most of all, ———— by the
applauses (loud and frequent) which remunerated
him for making faces and playing the buffoon. At
breakfast this morning, a flash or two, a recitation,
and a remark or two, and the charm was to be dis-
solved, was to be exchanged for—London.

Amsterdam : June 6, 1810.

Any other man, my dear Merivale, but myself would
have been in England many weeks ago. No passport has arrived from Paris, and friends by the
dozen are lost in wonder that I should wish to
trust myself in the heart of our enemies when I
can so easily return to my own country. . . . . I have
a natural antipathy to Trade—to what is trading,
has been trading, or shall or will be trading. And
so, having said that the country of Batavia—

Hollow-land, Holland — is a land very extraordinary—that to see a people give birth to their
country, instead of a country giving birth to the
people, is very odd and very creditable to the above
people—that the cities of Amsterdam, Hague,
Rotterdam, with many others, are the most this,
that, and t'other—that their inhabitants are respectable fair-dealing men, etc.—most gladly would I
bid them adieu for ever, go to some bastardly spot
of Provence, and vintage-think at my ease among
these modern Babylonians—for such, no doubt,
the whole French nation are—look at Faber else,
and the Prophecies which are literally fulfilling
before our faces.   This being the case, as it really
is, I shall follow the advice of a French gentleman,
who has been my friend in everything, and through
whom I have refrained from trusting myself as far
as Brussels without my viaticum—by remaining
here about ten days longer, in the almost certainty
of getting my passport; or, should it fail, with the
resolution to return among you—a resolution not
of my dictation, but that of necessity.

You have often scoffed and jeered and otherwise maltreated me for my love of harmony—
witness that celestial poem, the 'Four Slaves
which I hold to be pure music; that is, English

music. Well, sir, this unfortunate love, with a predilection for everything sunny and sweet, has prevented me from learning one word of German; so that, although one half of the superior commonalty here are Germans, I have not even had the curiosity to go once to their theatre.

. . . . The Germans are, doubtless, personally speaking, what the French call *faits à peindre.* Their regiments are really beautiful, and the young men of that nation, who are to be found everywhere, are of an exterior superior to any I have ever seen. They are generally accomplished in some two or three living languages, which they speak equally well with the natives. They are all musicians—they ride with a grace and agility which surprises—they are travellers—liberal in the highest degree; but are cursed with a jargon which, when they speak it, does away with all their excellencies. They are extremely loquacious and lively. How comes it that the French, who literally take no pains with themselves, are so completely their superiors? Sense, my friend; plain, natural, common understanding, unfettered by schools and metaphysical jargon, and the balderdash of Gottingen and other places, where such severe trials are made on weak human brains. The

next superiority is that honest and lively prepossession
for their country which the former are too *liberal*
to entertain. A German with whom I am here
very intimate has been coaxing me to learn the
language, under the promise of surprisingly beautiful thoughts in their poetry. May be so; they
resemble a surprisingly beautiful female clad in
bear-skin. Besides having made a vow to read
nothing but what is new, I have, in consequence,
determined to read no poetry but my own. Now
this is but natural; and then, to say the truth, I
hate poetry (always excepting my own) to such a
point that I shall manage to take a course of
French literature without the nausea of Corneille
and Racine. No: little Historical pieces, with which
they abound; Memoirs, in which they excel all
other nations for two reasons: first, because the
life of a French child is more chequered with
oddities than that of an English adventurer; and
secondly, because what is wanted to make Truth
interesting is supplied to the life from a quarter
opposite to Truth. These reasons, I say, make
their biography delicious.

Do not talk about translations for the stage.
I write no more, except in my own calling as a
clergyman; and, when I return, my whole aim will

be to gain something like an establishment in the Church. My appointment here has done for me great and unexpected things. The sinecure of £100 per annum, Merivale, is great for a Bland, or the son of a Bland. Besides, I have once been taken by the hand by Mr. Henry Hope, and led by him to a Bishop. Now had I taken Mr. H. H., or the said Bishop, by the hand and done him some service, I should have nothing to expect from them, because, as Sterne says, we get on in the world by receiving, not by doing, favours. You plant a tree, and, because you planted it, you water it. Thus, you see, I live in the frequent hope of being watered by a Bishop and by the greatest merchant in the world. In short, I shall state to the Bishop that a chapel in London (the word 'chapel' read in any sense you will) would be highly acceptable; that I am utterly disengaged; that I have all the wills in the world, and can get a character from my last place. Thus, between ourselves, Merry, I shall not be again the outcast that I have been. No; no more writing. Our 'Anthology,' our dear 'Anthology,' shall receive our united efforts. If you apply to William Harness (Berkeley Street) you may get dozens of my new pieces; Yatman has one or two; Mrs.

Burnley has a great number; my sister a few;
Denman (to whom I wrote two months ago a very
long letter) a few; Dr. Drury (to whom I wrote
an almost endless letter) has one or two. Have
you read my 'Origin of Snoring'? No, no more
reviewing for me, my friend. In short, no more
scribbling of any kind except in the way of a
clergyman, and conjointly with you a finish to the
'Anthology,' and by myself a thorough revisal of
my last romance, and the lopping the buffooneries
as much as possible, expunging harsh words, and
substituting softer sounds, cutting off the accursed
s from every word when it is possible without
great damage to the sense; nay, getting rid of it at
all events, and writing a long and learned preface
on tale-writing. No; on no consideration will I
write or translate. The drama is detestable, and,
after the French company, I shall despise our
stage more and more. No, they can do nothing.
The French are born actors. Who said that
Farce is unknown to the French? I beg leave to
state that from genteel comedy (which, with us,
meant that jackdaw, old Palmer, by way of gentleman, and that rushlight, Miss Farren, by way of a
lady), that from genteel comedy in all its shades
to the broadest farce, I can institute not a moment's

comparison between the best of our actors and the second best of theirs. Name me one single woman who enjoys the combined advantages of youth, beauty, exact proportions, grace, a sweet voice, various expression, *naïveté*, and aptness of falling into her several characters, on the whole English stage. Name me one single man (except Dowton) who can make you laugh without an effort either at grimacing with his voice or his face. What was that pompous, strutting, motherly woman, Mrs. Siddons, out of Lady Macbeth? Was she not *always* Lady Macbeth? Mrs. Jordan was a model of English elocution. Barring her singing (which, to my ear, was execrable), the organs of her voice were formerly the purest I ever heard, and, were she now young, I should consider her as the perfection of English utterance. Her acting should be my school so far as regarded sound. But, then, how totally deficient in grace, in all sovereign grace! True, she acted the country-girl—and so does Mdlle. d'Angeville at this place. Mercy! what a difference between the Hoyden rusticity of the one and the Air de Paysanne of the other! In everything the stage should present ornament. A drunken man may stagger, but grace should accompany him, even to the last extremity.   The rags of a beggar should not be revolting.   A deshabille—an everything—should be raised in its value, and *is* raised by the French to consequence by a certain style and *tournure*, of which our actors and their chubby dumplings of spouses are wholly unconscious.   The French possess another advantage—in face.   Persons who accidentally see a poor set of old abbés living in contempt and exile in the alleys of London, fancy them to be representatives of the French.   You have, in London, no conception of *youth*, when attached to the word 'French.'   On the Continent they are now in high feather—well-dressed, with good linen, and respected in every place.   The impressions here are, therefore, diametrically opposite to those in London.   Their face and figure are completely theatrical, and adapt themselves with ease to their several parts.

The next letter is written from London, after his return, in the language of the country to which he was so devotedly attached, and through which he had recently been making so perilous a tour. It contains some witty references to a recent review of his own writings, and those of Hodgson and Merivale, the latter of whom had just published

a third canto in continuation of Beattie's 'Minstrel.'[1]
The review considered that Merivale had improved
upon Beattie, and expressed a warm appreciation of
Hodgson's powers as a poet. The remaining extracts, which are from letters written at Kenilworth
between the years 1816 and 1820, contain the writer's
sentiments on country life in general and his own in
particular, together with fragmentary references to
literary subjects of mutual interest.

Here (he writes) we have a famous garden, shady
lanes and walks in all their intricacies, and abound-
ing in little surprises of views, a very fair (it is even
reckoned capital) neighbourhood, i.e. in a circle
whose radius is five miles. Castles entire and in
ruins, good modern dwellings, fertility, Dr. Parr,
Denman's fame in all its odour at the Warwick
Assizes, Leamington the salubrious, Coventry the
manufacturing, disgusting, dishonest, Warwick the
gallant, etc., etc., etc. All which being the case,
I will come and settle myself in Baker Street,
Portman Square, with the first puff of wind that
blows me £15,000. And yet, for *country*, this is
really very good. Its only harm, or rather vice, is
that it *is* country.

<hr>

[1] Longmans, 1808.

I have seldom left a house with such regret as I did yours. At the mercy of *respectable country society* whenever I sally from my own home (which is rarely, and against my wish), I leave it to you to judge how new, how surprising, how entertaining, improving, nay, how impossible the resources seem to me of a London party; the anecdote, wit, good taste, right feeling, politeness, good faith, confidence, that form the elements of London societies, and, to complete the panegyric, the total absence of all *respectability*, are really my astonishment. I touched, and only touched, on your coming to see me. I have no prospect of any other mode of meeting. Stay. Kenilworth, and indeed the tract from Coventry to the Vale of Evesham, is so pretty that it just touches on the beautiful without attaining it. My house—would it were mine!—is, with its present improvements, a very comfortable and convenient sort of mansion. Add to this, I have been gradually amassing from five to six hundred volumes, my only, and my absolutely necessary expense. I have much delight in contemplating my shelves, and the utility of them I daily feel. The walks around are good enough, the people exorbitantly rich and poor to the most degrading excess. Among the former, several good-doing busy-bodies, the heroes of vestries, givers of Bibles, occasionally of soup, and tolerable be-praisers of their own munificence. Among the latter, that complete *adscriptio glebæ*, that utter dependence and want of all pride and possession, which are totally incompatible with moral feeling. The great say: 'Give them Bibles, and more Bibles.' I say: 'Give each man the absolute proprietorship of his home, and a couple of acres of land, and his pride and its concomitant virtues will return.' In short, will you come and see me at Easter?

Ever and sincerely yours,

R. BLAND.

Kenilworth : April 2, 1819.

. . . . . The danger of our situation is in the necessity of keeping a good house and equipment at all times, and of living, when finances are low, in one equable train, and with a household mounted to correspond with far larger receipts. As for the occupation itself—*ille ego quem nôsti*—with all my inequalities, have managed to forge as few disagreeables to myself as any, the most cautious. The uncertainty of a sequence of *élèves* is our bitterest anxiety. If a man must live in the country with a London soul, why he might even as

well sit at home and talk of the darknesses of
Greek, as do anything else.   But of country-people
—the very poor—I do say, ' My soul, turn from
them !'

By the way, has Lord Byron published since
' Beppo' ?   Do desire the Murray, if you see him,
to send me his next work on its first coming out.
Thank you for talking of 'the ten,' and of maga-
zines and other puerilities, but *non eadem est ætas,
non mens.*   I have said my say to my uttermost
idea, and lo ! it is as if it were unsaid.   I have so all-
to-be-Greeked myself, that I am yet more stupid
than of old—an inconvenience somehow attached
to the study of the finest language in the world, and
from which none, without exception, who know
anything about it, can possibly escape. . . . I was
egregiously mistaken in believing that I could
lounge about London and Harrow, in the absence
of my wife and family.   The truth is, persons
whose existence are so monotonous, and arduous,
and so dreadfully precarious as ours, should not
separate.   I felt this last year—I felt it again this
—but, somehow, forgot to put it into the form
of a new observation.   Here then, ' what oft was
thought ' is at length expressed for the benefit of
the Universe.   In a word, I will never leave home

'to go a pleasuring,' as the servants say, without my wife, until I get so rich that these sicknesses of the soul shall have subsided.

In 1820, Merivale published a burlesque entitled 'Richardetto,'[1] and suggested by Hookham Frere's whimsical production 'Whistlecraft.' Of this poetical trifle Hodgson writes with appreciative warmth.

'Richardetto' I have received and read; laughed with and wondered at; sighed over, and laid down with mingled pleasure and vexation. This is the exact truth, but I shall not at present venture to interpret it. In this age of minute criticism, all the *little natural touches* (as they are called) cannot fail to be observed and extolled. Seriously, I think you much funnier than Whistlecraft. Bland is equally eulogistic.

Kenilworth: May 20, 1820.

My very dear Merivale,—Call me 'ungrateful, reprobate, degraded, spiritless outcast,' but never say I am forgetful—for the fact is, I have done, and still do, all in my power not to write to you or any one; and now, if I could be certain of sleeping if I left

---

[1] From an original poem of Nicolo Fortiguerra.

off, I would not add a word more. My opinion of
the state of things is this: you—*et vos semblables*,
if, *per hasard*, there exists a semblance in the
world—have too firmly convinced yourselves of the
excellence of Will Whistlecraft's performance,
which has a strong smack of that Italian cask,
always so palatable and pleasurable to yourself.
That is, *you* are a man of good present and future
fortunes. *I*, on the contrary, have much less than
no fortune at present, and see a further remove
from her favours in futurity. *You* are immersed
in the world, its gaieties, varieties, conversations,
contradictions, and acquaintances; whereas, *I* never
clash with, or meet, any world at all, except myself
at toilette, and even that fascination begins to tire.
Again, Nature may have possibly instilled into
your ——. No, no; *that* she has not, nor into any
one's veins, more milk of gentleness than into
mine. And so we will even keep to the difference
of fortunes, mixing in the world, admiration (even
to gloating) of Italian, and strong prepossession
for Will Whistlecraft; and these said circumstances
and feelings procreated, and otherwise engen-
dered, a better thing than Will's—most probably a
better thing than Fortiguerra's—but not so good a
thing as your own brains had reel'd, spun, and

woven, had your own brains really been consulted; the language plain, easy, and of most accessible construction—the stanza playful, and done evidently while you were whistling—in a word, facile to excess.   Much fun; but I vow you could, without a particle more pains, do a better thing.   I mean you might invent a more amusing story; and then all would be as it should be.   Have I wounded my brother?   Say no; for Heaven knows I have so few brothers in this world, that to me it is all a wilderness—even to this late day of my existence.

A few months before poor Bland's death, Hodgson wrote to Merivale about him with characteristic tenderness.

His weakness is extreme, and a return of his attack would too probably be fatal.   Who can guarantee him against it while his mind is the prey and sport of the most unhappy feelings?   Would to Heaven we could, any or all of us, devise some scheme to aid his retreating to a softer and more congenial air, with any prospect of employment and support!

The kind intention was too late to be of use, but

a fund was raised for the bereaved family, by contributing to which (some of them far beyond their means) his friends paid a touching tribute to his talents and to the kindly gentleness of his impulsive nature.

CHAPTER XII.

CORRESPONDENCE WITH DRURY AND MERIVALE—
A RUGBY EXAMINATION — ASSASSINATION OF
PERCEVAL—DUKE OF GLOUCESTER, CHANCELLOR
OF CAMBRIDGE — LETTER FROM LONSDALE —
'LEAVES OF LAUREL.'

1812-13.

THE digression in the last chapter seemed to be
justified, if not demanded, by the intimacy which
long existed between Bland and Hodgson, and by
the similarity of their literary tastes. It is now time
to resume the thread of correspondence with other
friends. The first of the following letters quaintly
describes the exhibition of the predecessor of the
great Madame Tussaud ; the next (in verse), vividly
depicts a public school examination at the commencement of the present century ; the third has
reference to a matter of national interest, the assassination of the Prime Minister in the House of
Commons.

To Mr. Henry Drury.

My dear Harry,—You have doubtless greatly enjoyed your Devonshire visit, notwithstanding your seclusion and most natural dislike to reviewing. I feel the latter dislike as much as you can, but, as to retirement, I confess a few friends and a cottage would be my *summum bonum*, could I command such blessings in the *environs of London*. It is not solitude, but knowing that you cannot have society, which is unpleasant. I will deliver your message about a Fen Scheme to Hart when I return to King's. Lonsdale is there at present, in very ill-health. . . . I write this from London, where I have come to meet my sister[1] from Kensington. I have been rambling about with her all the morning to see sights. Miss Linwood's worsted pictures, in which I think she has *worsted* all our painters, if you *canvass* her merits ever so severely. Bullock's Museum, a farrago of birds, beasts, snakes, shells, and butterflies ; and Mrs. Salmon's original and royal waxworks, where, in addition to the old curiosities (which I have not seen these twenty years, but well remember) there is the

---

[1] Afterwards married to her cousin the Rev. Geo. Coke, of Lemore, in Herefordshire.

Duchess of Brunswick, lying in state in a room lighted with wax tapers, with two waxen bishops at her head, a waxen Princess of Wales weeping over her, a wax waiting-woman, and a wax emblem of Peace, strewing flowers at her feet. Two wax mutes stand at the door of the chamber. Perhaps you have forgotten the room upstairs. Werter and Charlotte and the pistol were being cleaned; so was Buonaparte, and the lady who bled to death from pricking her finger while working on a Sunday; these interesting groups, therefore, were lost to us. But we saw Alexander, and the Queen of Darius and her waiting-maid, and the nurse on her knees begging the life of the prince, a fine chubby child, beside her; Alexander looks about sixty years of age, but perhaps he has grown old apace since I last saw him; and Antony and Cleopatra certainly have lost some of their youthful charms. But Mrs. Siddons's sister still begs as piteously as in life; and Mother Shipton (saving her leg, which is out of joint, and has ceased kicking) is as attractive as ever. Henderson in Macbeth must have been very grand. I took him at first for the beefeater that used to stand at the door. But, as Mr. Puff has it, 'I would not have you too sure he is a beefeater.' The lady abbess and her nuns, who slit their noses and lips to disgust the marauding Danes, and so preserve their virgin vows, are in full perfection, only I observed that neither their noses nor lips were slit; and the Lady Margaret of Holland is lying in bed as usual, just having produced her 365th child, according to the prayer of the beggar-woman whom her ladyship offended. The nun, the priest, the waiting-woman, all *wax* sorrowful at her side. But perhaps you will say I am *cereus in vitium*, and so farewell for the present, and

Believe me, my dear Harry,

Ever yours affectionately,

FRANCIS HODGSON.

To Mrs. Coke.

To Rugby, dear aunt, I set out to go down,
At five on the evening of Friday from Town ;
From the Swan-with-two-Necks in Lad Lane I set out,
And a numerous party within and without.
I roof'd it myself, and it rain'd very hard,
But I laugh'd through the night at the jokes of the guard.
On my life, of all wits the completest and best
Is the guard of that coach for original jest;
For free illustration of easy remark,
And all that enlivens a drive in the dark.
By six in the morning to Dunchurch we came,
To the sign of 'The Cow' with the terrible name;

Here I hasten'd to bed, and slept soundly till four,
Seven hours of good rest, or perchance somewhat more.
Like the lark, or the nightingale rather, I rose,
And put on my best suit of examining clothes.
In my chariot and pair to the Doctor's I rode,
And was kindly received at his courteous abode.
That my story's detail may be thoroughly full,
I must tell you the name of the Doctor is Wooll. [1]
Mrs. Wooll and her sister, the Doctor and I,—
But to business of greater importance I fly.
Our sermon on Sunday from good Mr. Heath
Might have come from the lips of the Bishop of Meath ;
But I thought it a custom exceedingly queer
That the boys in the church should cry out 'We are here.'
For the muster-roll's called, and I fancied, for one,
That it better had anywhere else have been done.
And the organ, though rightly to fiddles preferr'd,
Was the loudest and harshest I ever had heard.
But this I pass over—for, eager to praise,
I banish all satire and spleen from my lays.
Doctor Wooll and myself were in close tête-à-tête
How the Oxford Examiner could be so late,
When he came in his gig, just in time to prevent
My taking both places with perfect content.
On Monday at nine our proceedings began
(Mr. H., like myself, is a grave sort of man),

---

[1] Dr. Wooll, a pedagogue of diminutive stature and pompous presence, was once showing an old gentleman over the school buildings, when he came upon the room where his pupils underwent the extreme penalty of the law 'This,' exclaimed the doctor with great magnificence, 'is my flogging-room.' 'Oh,' replied the *irreverent* senior, 'then I suppose that here there must be great cry and little Wooll.'

And till four the poor boys, with but small intermission,
Were compell'd to write verses with speed and precision.
On Tuesday again all the morning we sate,
Trustees and examiners deep in debate ;
The latter in gowns, like inquisitors drest,
In boots and in riding apparel the rest.
The boys answer'd well every question we put,
Till their books and our own with like pleasure were shut.
Then we feasted on venison and capital fare,
Lord Ailsford, our president, sate in the chair,
And many of equal distinction were there.
Sir Theophilus Biddulph, and Skipwith Sir Grey,
(Lord Craven, for some proper cause, kept away),
Lord Wentworth, Grimes, Digby, and Holbeach, Esquires,
The last, Mr. Trevor's old friend, and my sire's ;
Dr. Berkeley, and others—a company staunch
As ever sate down to a pasty and haunch.
For myself I was glad that our business was done,
And some moments allowed to good humour and fun ;
But still better pleased, that the boys, by their knowledge,
Had three of them gained exhibitions at college ;
And beginning their race with some marks of renown,
Might perchance to the goal with like honour go down.

From Mr. Merivale.

My dear Hodgson,—Thank you for being the first to
break the inhuman silence of which you so justly
complain.   Ever since you wrote, I have been very
uncomfortable at home in consequence of another
illness of my wife.   With this, and a good deal of

business at chambers, I have had as little time as spirits to write, though, on Tuesday, I should certainly have done so, in order to communicate the bloody business [1] of the preceding evening, if I had not been interrupted by Ben Drury's arrival, and gone down with him to the House of Commons, where we were both highly gratified by the conduct of the whole House on this unexampled occasion. Whitbread did himself immortal honour by his manly and generous speech. Ponsonby's totally unaffected feelings so overcame him as greatly to interrupt and cut short his rhetoric; but the effect was, of course, so much the more impressive. Even Lord Castlereagh, aye, the Castlereagh of Walcheren, the Castlereagh of Ireland, I adored at the moment. Canning was the only man that spoke who had sufficient command of himself to attempt turning a sentence prettily; and his speech, accordingly, was very pretty indeed. As for Burdett, poor miserable creature as he is, his silence now has, I think, sunk him lower than his noise heretofore. Suppose for a moment that Pitt had been assassinated like Perceval, and that the savage mob had mingled the cry of 'Fox for ever'

---

[1] The assassination of Perceval, then Prime Minister, by Bellingham, within the walls of the House.

with their brutal exultations, would he not have made all Westminster ring—

and more,

From Tothill Fields to Lambeth's Surrey shore,

with the vehemence of his generous execrations of the deed ? As for his pitiful successor, he is too mean-spirited for a decided villain ; and accordingly I do not believe that he exulted, like his own miserable electors, in the deed. But that he did not rush forward at the instant to disavow it and declare his abhorrence of the wretches who could use his name on such an occasion, and his deep sorrow that in the discharge of his public duty he should ever have used expressions capable of such inflammatory interpretation, such horrible mis-construction ; this, I think, is enough to rank him with Philippe Egalité himself.

And now that we are able to take breath, and ask ourselves, what will be the probable result of this 'knavish piece of work,' I am greatly afraid, for my own part, that there is little room for hope of ultimate good. 'The Church was cemented by the blood of its martyrs,' and, unfortunately, whether a cause is good or bad, these violent acts of revenge and desperation against its supporters are, I believe, uniformly found rather to benefit than to injure it. If I am not mistaken, the universal feeling of pity and horror for the deed, and of apprehension for its consequences, will strengthen the hands of the present Government, notwithstanding the loss of its chief, even more than the most rigorous exertions of Perceval, when alive, could have done it. I anticipate no speedy change, either of men or measures, as its consequence ; and, if there is none, what have we to do but deplore, without any mixture of hope or satisfaction, the loss of a man, who, however erroneous his principles, was a man of business, of firmness, and integrity, far superior to any of those with whom he was associated in power?

I have not a moment's time to write any further. You have heard of the birth of Drury's son. When do you leave Cambridge? I wish to my soul that we could meet. Write directly if you can furnish me with any plan of your operations.

Yours ever affectionately,

J. H. MERIVALE.

In the election of the Duke of Gloucester in 1811 to the Chancellorship of the University of Cambridge Hodgson took an active part, as is proved by two letters—one from that Edward Dwyer, upon whom Byron elsewhere begs Drury to execute summary punishment 'for frightening his horses with his flame-coloured whiskers,' the other from the Duke's private secretary.

My dear Hodgson,—Ten thousand thanks for your very kind letter, which I have transmitted to the Duke, who, I am sure, will consider himself under no small obligation, not only for the very handsome manner in which you support him, but also for the valuable intelligence of the state of parties which it conveys. I officiate to-morrow at Lincoln's Inn, both morning and evening, but intend, if I have time, to see the Duke, and the moment I have anything to communicate I shall transmit it to you, whom we may regard as one of our main pillars. I saw our friend Drury on Thursday, and am chagrined to find that the report of his preferment is without foundation.

Yours ever,
EDWARD DWYER.

Sir,—I am honoured with the commands of His Royal Highness the Duke of Gloucester to return to you his best thanks, with an assurance His

Royal Highness entertains of your attention to him in the election to the Chancellorship.

I have the honour to be, Sir,

Your very obedient and humble servant,

EDMUND CURREY.

The interest which Hodgson took in this election, like all other subjects which interested him, found an utterance in verses. In an irregular ode for the installation of the Duke of Gloucester, a sketch is given of all the most illustrious Cambridge students who had passed the lamp of genius on from one generation to another.

The youthful characteristics of a future Bishop of Lichfield of such eminence as Lonsdale, and his views on various subjects, are *pro tanto* instructive.

Harrow: March 12.

My dear Hodgson,—Requested or rather commanded by the great, I write to request your 'vote and interest' for the Duke of Rutland and Lord Palmerston. The latter I conceive you will oppose *from principle.* . . . . Lonsdale has just left me: he is a most excellent, clever, and affable fellow. I am highly delighted with him. You will see him at Cambridge in a day or two; when, I hope, he will be able to arrange something with you touching the Easter holidays. My plans are not yet made up; but my wavering is in consequence of your delay in settling. Lonsdale is my agent to treat with you: he and I will meet you anywhere. In haste.

Most truly yours,

H. DRURY.

Dear Hodgson,—I must allow the justice of the complaints of your third letter against me for not having sooner thanked you for the pleasure which I received from your two first, poetical as they were; and for so long omitting to acknowledge the receipt of the enclosed unpoetical scraps of paper, which by reunion to one another have been sometime restored to that consequence in the world of which their separation deprived them. But I hope that you will not suffer your anger to proceed so far against me as to forbid your muse to address any more of her effusions to me: still less am I disposed to think that, when you say that you 'must not sing again at all,' your declaration is any other than merely poetical.

Oh, never check thy flowing strain,
Nor say, ' I must not sing again.'
Whate'er the tenour of thy lay,
Serenely sad, or wildly gay ;
Whether 'tis Love that wakes to fire
The slumb'ring raptures of thy lyre ;
Or Reason bids the moral song
In sober cadence roll along ;
Believe me, still to Friendship's ear
Thy strain is sweet, thy muse is dear.
Oh ! better far one verse of thine,
One artless bold, impassion'd line,
Than all the frigid rant, that e'er
Fitzgerald bawls or Tories hear,
What time to Bigotry's blest pow'r
They dedicate the festal hour
And raise their heads in triumph high
O'er baffled Liberality ;
Who weeps the while at Fox's tomb,
And thinks on happier days to come.

You see how I, albeit unused to the rhyming mood, have been infected by the contagion of your example. But ' ohe jam satis est '—' neque enim concludere versum Dixeris esse satis.'—You ask me what I am doing here. Truth compels me to answer next to nothing ; for the fact is that I find that unless I am actually tied down to some employment it is impossible to prefer dry reading to social pleasure. When I return to town after the summer,

if I do return, I am determined to go immediately
to a special pleader, by which I shall be put into a
train of doing something, and fall into the habit of
business, if anything can counteract the effects of
the desultory manner in which everything is done
at Eton and King's. Since we parted I have been
present at some Harrow speeches, which are far
superior to those at Eton, even if the entertainment
after them be not considered. I have also been
spending a day or two with B. Drury at Eton, who
brought me back in his curricle by way of Richmond on Saturday. The day was fine, and consequently I cannot say how beautiful I thought that
place. Eton looks all lovely, always excepting
Carter's chamber, which is more beastly than
ever.

Believe me, dear Hodgson, very sincerely yours,
JNO. LONSDALE.

In the spring of this year, the Laureateship having
fallen vacant by the death of poet Pye, Hodgson published a series of imitations of living poets, in the
style of the 'Rejected Addresses' which had appeared
in the previous autumn. They are entitled 'Leaves of
Laurel,' or 'New Probationary Odes for the vacant
Laureateship,' and are prefaced by the Miltonian

motto, 'Yet once more, oh ye laurels,' &c. The judge of the rival performances is supposed to be the celebrated clown Grimaldi, whose successive criticisms are singularly appropriate. Campbell and Rogers commence the competition, and the 'Pleasures of Hope' are aptly contrasted with the 'Pleasures of Memory.' By a sudden transition Scott supplants the rivals, and full justice is done to the extreme beauty of his descriptive powers, while the rapidity of his execution is very cleverly parodied. Byron follows, and in a mournful monologue bewails the nothingness of all earthly existence, where 'dust is all in all, and all in all is dust.' His inordinate fondness for that poetical device which he used himself to term 'alliteration's apt and artful aid,' and his habit of introducing obsolete words and phrases, were often the subjects of good-humoured banter among his friends, and are here amusingly ridiculed. Moore continues the contest with an eulogy of Dryden in the metre of 'Love's Young Dream,' and is followed by Crabbe, whom the judge pronounces to be Nature itself, and by Wordsworth, whose simplicity is declared to exceed even that of Nature. After the introduction of several minor poets, the Resurrection Tragedy by Coleridge, and Southey's 'Blessings of a Sinecure' conclude the series

The ' Leaves of Laurel ' were much discussed and admired in literary society at the time of their publication, and, as in the case of the ' Rejected Addresses,' the poets whose style they imitated were not the last to appreciate their spirit and humour.

CHAPTER XIII.

INTENDED MARRIAGE — BYRON'S GENEROSITY --
LETTERS FROM BYRON, ROGERS, PRINCE LUCIEN
BUONAPARTE, MRS. LEIGH, AND MISS MILBANKE.

1813-14.

IN this and the following year (1813-14) Hodgson
spent the greater part of his Cambridge vacations in
London, where he was pretty constantly in the company of Lord Byron, and was cordially admitted into
that brilliant society, of which those who had opportunities of contemporary observation have declared
that it has never been surpassed. Holland House
opened its hospitable doors to him, and he was
brought into close contact with many of those
stars of the literary firmament whose brightness
shed undying lustre upon the age in which they
shone.

There is unfortunately no detailed record of this
most interesting period of his life ; but the ensuing
letters testify sufficiently to the high estimation in

which his character and talents were held by two at least of his associates, whose praise was fame.

It was most unfortunate that at this very time those pecuniary embarrassments, to which allusion has previously been made, were pressing most heavily upon him—embarrassments from which he was suddenly relieved in a manner equally unsolicited and unexpected. It was in the autumn of the first of these years that Byron gave proof of the depth of his regard for his friend, no less than of the natural nobility of his disposition, by his generous gift of 1,000*l.* Hodgson had become attached to a Miss Tayler, a young lady of great beauty and refinement, whose sister was married to his old friend and school-fellow, Henry Drury. The mother refused her consent to the marriage unless all previous liabilities were completely cleared. Byron at once offered to discharge his friend's debts—an offer which Hodgson, after repeated refusals, ultimately accepted, although he resolved to consider the assistance as merely temporary, as a loan rather than a gift.

In a letter to his uncle, the Rev. Francis Coke, written in November of this year, Hodgson thus comments upon this signal instance of true friendship :—

My noble-hearted friend Lord Byron, after many

offers of a similar kind, which I felt bound to re-
fuse, has irresistibly in my present circumstances
(as I will soon explain to you) volunteered to pay
all my debts, and within a few pounds it is done!
Oh, if you knew (but *you* do know) the exaltation
of heart, aye and of head too, I feel, at being free
from these depressing embarrassments, you would,
as I do, bless my dearest friend and brother Byron.
And what has made me now accept what I have
before frequently declined?

Then he goes on to declare his engagement, to
which reference has been made above. The friends
went together in Lord Byron's carriage to Hammers-
ley's in Pall Mall, where the money was transferred
from one account to the other. 'On our way back
to his lodgings' (in Bennet Street), Hodgson writes,
'I expressed as well as I could (and it was not very
easy), my overwhelming gratitude; and he replied,
with the strongest marks of feeling, and disinclination
to hear the thing mentioned, " Don't speak of it, I
always intended to do it." ' He seems only to have
waited for the opportunity when the gift would be of
greatest service. Nothing can exceed the delicacy of
feeling, the tender consideration displayed by Byron
on this occasion. But, notwithstanding the repeated

assurances of the donor, the sense of obligation appears to have continued to weigh heavily upon the recipient for many months, during which he more than once offered bonds and promissory notes bearing interest, all of which Byron resolutely refused, with such words as these: 'What is the use of a bond? I should only destroy or cancel it, or leave you the same by will.'

Some years afterwards Bland wrote on this subject:—

I remember distinctly, and as if it were yesterday, sitting with Byron one day, at his lodgings in the street going into St. James's Street, when, in one of his lighter moods, he was talking you over. Among other pleasantries he spoke with great glee upon the idea of your ever refunding; with some tenderness on his ever re-accepting what he had given; and then glee again upon your having put or thrust or shoved (for this was his style) a paper into his hands which he destroyed, saying: 'As if I ought to have given it him on such terms, as if I would ever listen to such nonsense, as if anyone knowing Hodgson's finances could dream of such a thing.'

At the end of November 1813, it became known

to Byron that Hodgson, in the fulness of his gratitude, had mentioned the present to mutual friends ; and on December 1, Byron writes, apologising for the fact of his assistance being known to a person whom he mentions, or to anyone save Drury and Hodgson himself, who, he is sure, 'cannot be more hurt at it than he is himself ;' and adds : ' If you ever considered it in the least an obligation, this must give you a full and fair release from it,' finishing jocosely, as was his wont, but not the less feelingly,

> To John I owe some obligation,
> But John unluckily thinks fit
> To publish it to all the nation,
> So John and I are more than quit.

In his diary, written the same night, we read :—

Wrote to H. He has been telling that I ———. I am sure, at least, I did not mention it, and I wish he had not. He is a good fellow, and I obliged myself ten times more by being of use than I did him,—and there's an end on't.

Curiously enough, notwithstanding Byron's impression that he had destroyed them all, one of Hodgson's promissory notes did slip into the memoranda and letters left by the noble poet at his death, and upon this unexpectedly discovered document the executors set up a claim for repayment, which, however, as soon as the real nature of the transaction became apparent, was at once relinquished.

In October 1813, Byron, Drury, and Hodgson went together in a postchaise to Oxford, where Byron had an interview with Mrs. Tayler, who was then on a visit to her brother, the Dean of Christ Church. The result of this interview was the removal of all objections to the intended marriage, which, however, did not take place until the beginning of the next year but one. Hodgson waited in the expectation of a college living; but, as none appeared likely to fall vacant, he married on a curacy, and soon afterwards obtained a living through private interest. These successive events will be duly chronicled in the order of their occurrence. In the meantime, the correspondence of the current year demands insertion. The first letter refers to a previous proposal by Hodgson that the intended gift should be a loan.

February 3, 1813.

My dear Hodgson,—I will join you in any bond for the money you require, be it that or a larger sum. With regard to security, as Newstead is in a sort of abeyance between sale and purchase, and my

Lancashire property very unsettled, I do not know how far I can give more than personal security, but what I can I will. I hear nothing of my own concerns, but expect a letter daily. Let me hear from you where you are and will be this month. I am a great admirer of the R. A. ('Rejected Addresses'), though I have had so great a share in the cause of their publication, and I like the C. H. ('Childe Harold') imitation one of the best. Lady O. (Oxford) has heard me talk much of you as a relative of the Cokes, etc., and desires me to say she would be happy to have the pleasure of your acquaintance. You must come and see me at K——. I am sure you would like *all* here if you knew them.

The 'Agnus'[1] is furious. You can have no idea of the horrible and absurd things she has said and done since (really from the best motives) I withdrew my homage. 'Great pleasure' is, certes, my object, but ' *Why brief*, Mr. Wild ?' I cannot answer for the future, but the past is pretty secure ; and in it I can number the last two months as worthy of the gods in *Lucretius*. I cannot review in the ' Monthly ;' in fact I can just now do nothing,

---

[1] Lady Caroline Lamb.

at least with a pen ; and I really think the days of authorship are over with me altogether. I hear and rejoice in Bland's and Merivale's intentions.[1] Murray has grown great, and has got him new premises in the fashionable part of town. We live here so shut out of the *monde* that I have nothing of general import to communicate, and fill this up with a 'happy new year,' and drink to you and Drury.

Ever yours, dear H.,

B.

I have no intention of continuing 'Childe Harold.' There are a few additions in the ' body of the book ' of description, which will merely add to the number of pages in the next edition. I have taken Thyrnham Court. The business of last summer I broke off, and now the amusement of the gentle fair is writing letters literally threatening my life, and much in the style of Miss Matthews in 'Amelia,' or Lucy in the 'Beggar's Opera.' Such is the reward of restoring a woman to her family, who are treating her with the greatest kindness, and with whom I am on good terms. I am still in ' palatia Circes,' and, being no Ulysses, cannot tell

---

[1] The republication of the *Anthology*.

into what animal I may be converted. . . . . She
has had her share of the denunciations of the
brilliant Phryne, and regards them as much as I
do. I hope you will visit me at Th., which will not
be ready before spring, and I am very sure you
would like my neighbours if you knew them. If
you come down now to Kington,[1] pray come and
see me.

June 6, 1813.

My dear Hodgson,—I write to you a few lines on
business. Murray has thought proper at his own
risk, and peril, and profit (if there be any) to
publish the 'Giaour'; and it may possibly come
under your ordeal in the 'Monthly.' I merely wish
to state that in the published copies there are
additions to the amount of ten pages, *text* and
margin (*chiefly* the last), which render it a little less
unfinished (but more unintelligible) than before.
If, therefore, you review it, let it be from the published copies and not from the first sketch. I shall
not sail for this month, and shall be in town again
next week, when I shall be happy to hear from
but more glad to see you. You know I have no

---

[1] Near Lower Moor, the residence of his relatives, the Cokes.

time or turn for correspondence (!).   But you also
know, I hope, that I am not the less

Yours ever,

ΜΠΑΙΡΩΝ.

The first of the two following letters from Mr.
Samuel Rogers was written in acknowledgment of a
letter expressing admiration of his last poem 'Co-
lumbus ;' the second has reference to Merivale's
'Richardetto,' which has been noticed in a former
chapter :—

My dear Sir,—What shall I say to you for your very
kind and encouraging letter ?   I can assure you I
opened it at a moment when it would affect me
the most ; and, whatever the critics may say, I
shall always regard it as a much higher reward.
Praise such as yours is what I have always wished
for above all things, though I fear I never shall
deserve it.

With the greatest respect,

I am yours most sincerely,

SAML. ROGERS.

My dear Sir,—Many, many thanks for your kindness,
and pray express my grateful acknowledgments to
Mr. Merivale for his very elegant present.   I make

no doubt that it will fulfill (*sic*) your promise—that
I shall read it with my first feelings—and that it
will bring back to my mind that delicious evening
(an evening in July) when I first discovered the
'Minstrel'[1] among some loose pamphlets in my
father's library. Alas! alas! Five and thirty
years have fled, and yet it seems but yesterday.

Yours most sincerely,

SAML. ROGERS.

From Lord Byron.

October 1, 1813.

My dear H.,—I leave town again for Aston[2] on
Sunday, but have messages for you. Lord Holland
desired me repeatedly to bring you; he wants to
know you much, and begged me to say so; you
will like him. I had an invitation for you to
dinner there this last Sunday, and Rogers is per-
petually screaming because you don't call, and
wanted you also to dine with him on Wednesday
last. Yesterday we had Curran there—who is
beyond all conception!—and Mackintosh and the
wits are to be seen at H. H. constantly, so that I

---

[1] By Beattie.

[2] Aston Hall, near Rotherham, Yorkshire, now the property of
Harry Verelst, Esq., brother-in-law to the writer of this memoir.

think you would like their society. I will be a judge between you and the attorned. So B.[1] may mention me to Lucien if he still adheres to his opinion. Pray let Rogers be one ; he has the best taste extant. Bland's nuptials delight me ; if I had the least hand in bringing them about it will be a subject of selfish satisfaction to me these three weeks. Desire Drury—if he loves me—to kick Dwyer thrice for frightening my horses with his flame-coloured whiskers last July. Let the kicks be hard, etc.

On his return from Aston a fortnight later he adds a hurried apology for the brevity of his letters at this time.

Excuse haste and laconism. I am in town but for a few days, and hurried with a thousand things.
        Believe me ever yours most truly,
                BYRON.

The Lucien referred to above is Prince Lucien Buonaparte, who had recently published an epic poem, in twenty-four books, entitled 'Charlemagne ; or, the Church Delivered,' the translation of which

---

[1] Butler.

was undertaken by the Rev. Samuel Butler, Head-Master of Shrewsbury, and Francis Hodgson. Of part of the latter's share in the work, the 'Critical' remarks that it combines closeness with luminous force.

The following letter proves that the appreciation of his talents as a translator was not confined to English readers :—

20 octobre 1813.

Monsieur,—Je reçois avec reconnaissance le bel exemplaire de votre traduction de Juvenal : je ne suis pas en état de juger de la poésie anglaise, mais l'opinion publique sur votre ouvrage est la garantie de ce que vous ferez pour Charlemagne : j'ai reçu des lettres de M. le docteur Parr et du chevalier (Boothby ?), qui parlent tous de vous comme M.' Butler, et, comme j'en pense, d'après notre promenade en enfer : à propos d'enfer, je viens de faire un changement à la décoration du bouclier d'Ir-mensul[1] dans le 10me Chant. Au lieu d'un Léopard farouche lisez d'un Dragon furieux : le léopard est sur les armes d'une nation trop civilisée et trop respectée par moi, quoique momentairement [2]

---

[1] Under the character of Irmensul, the god of the Saxons and northern hordes, the miraculous agency of Satan is introduced into the poem.

[2] Illegible.

pour que nous le laissions sur le bouclier d'Ir-
mensul. Agréez mes compliments affect. Votre
très, etc.

LUCIEN BUONAPARTE.

The poem of 'Charlemagne' was begun on the
mountains of Tusculum, near Rome, where the
Prince had retired after having quitted public affairs ;
it was continued at Malta, and finished during its
author's captivity in England. The dedication to
Pope Pius VII. was written at Rome in May 1814,
in grateful recognition of the kindnesses with which
His Holiness had loaded the Prince and his family
for ten years.

In Byron's journal and letters of this year there
are some general remarks on several characteristic
traits of Hodgson's disposition, which bear interesting
testimony to the value attached to his opinion on
literary subjects, and to the warm affection which
existed between them.   For instance, in a letter to
Murray, after a complaint of the unexpected length
to which the 'Giaour' had been extended, the poet
observes :—

The last lines Hodgson likes. It is not often he does,
    and when he don't he tells me with great energy,
    and I fret and alter.

To Moore he writes :—

I hope you are going on with your *grand coup*.[1] Pray do ; or that ——— Lucien Buonaparte will beat us all. I have seen much of his poem in MS., and he really surpasses everything beneath Tasso. Hodgson is translating him against another bard. You (and I believe Rogers), Scott, Gifford, and myself are to be referred to as judges between the twain.

In the journal for November 1813, we read :—

Hodgson, too, came. He is going to be married, and he is the kind of man who will be happier. He has talent, cheerfulness, everything that can make him a pleasing companion ; and his intended is handsome and young and all that.

Again, of the 'Bride of Abydos,' he says :—

Hodgson likes it better than the 'Giaour,' but nobody else will ; and he never liked the 'Fragment.'

And, again, in the same month, in a letter to Murray :—

Mr. Hodgson has looked over and stopped (or, rather,

[1] *Lalla Rookh.*

pointed) this revise, which must be the one to print from. He has also made some suggestions, with most of which I have complied, as he has always, for these ten years, been a very sincere and by no means (at times) flattering critic of mine. He likes it (you will think flatteringly in this instance) better than the 'Giaour,' but doubts (and so do I) its being so popular ; but, contrary to some others, advises a separate publication. On this we can easily decide. I confess I like the *double* form better. Hodgson says it is better versified than any of the others, which is odd, if true, as it has cost me less time (though more hours at a time) than any attempt I ever made.

Hodgson was among those favoured few to whom Murray received special instructions to send the earliest copies. His opinion of the ' Bride ' was soon endorsed by no less a personage than Canning, who pronounced it to be ' very, very beautiful.' Six thousand copies were sold in one month. As a striking instance of the retentiveness of its author's memory, it may here be mentioned that he once recited it from beginning to end whilst travelling with Hodgson in a post-chaise by night from Newstead to London.

In February of the following year the Journal continues :—

Hodgson just called and gone. He has much *bon-hommie* with his other good qualities, and more talent than he has yet had credit for beyond his circle.

And again :—

I wish that I had a talent for the drama; I would write a tragedy *now*. But no, it is gone. Hodgson talks of one—he will do it well; and I think Moore should try it.

The next letter from Byron, and the next from T. Rennell, a King's man of some reputation in his day, who was at this time a candidate for the Provostship of his College,[1] caused by the death of Humphrey Sumner, bear evidence to the feeling entertained by friends of the kindliness of Hodgson's nature.

Feb. 28, 1814.

There is a youngster, and a clever one, named Reynolds, who has just published a poem called 'Safia,' published by Cawthorne. He is in the most natural and fearful apprehension of the reviewers;

---

[1] Hodgson's support had already been given to his more intimate friend Geo. Thackeray, who was ultimately elected.

and as you and I both know by experience the effect of such things upon a *young* mind, I wish *you* would take his production into dissection, and do it gently. I cannot, because it is inscribed to me; but I assure you this is not my motive for wishing him to be tenderly entreated, but because I know the misery, at his time of life, of untoward remarks upon first appearance. Now for self. Pray thank your cousin; it is just as it should be, to my liking, and probably more than will suit anyone else's. I hope and trust you are well and well-doing.

Peace be with you !

Ever yours, my dear friend,
BYRON.

Deanery, Winton: March 26, 1814.

Dear Sir,—I fear you will think me very presumptuous, in placing myself before you as candidate for the succession to the Provostship of King's in the present vacancy. But as I thought I discerned, when I had the happiness of seeing you, that the 'elements were mixed in you,' and that a large portion of the milk of human kindness was combined with your other high talents and attainments, I trust that whatever may be the part

you take in this contest you will receive with
candour my application for your support.   Believe
me, sir, that I neither vapour nor flatter when I
say that I have both a mind to feel and gratitude
to appreciate the value of such support.   I can
only add that if by the kindness of my friends I
should succeed, my residence upon my post should
be constant, and that, in conjunction with yourself
and others animated by the same views, I should,
according to the best of my powers, endeavour to
encourage and promote a spirit of honourable
emulation and industry among the young men of
the College.

I beg you to believe me,

Yours with great esteem,

T. RENNELL.

It was in this year that Hodgson commenced a
correspondence with Lord Byron's sister, the Hon.
Mrs. Leigh, with whom he had for some time been
acquainted ; a correspondence which was continued
at frequent intervals for nearly forty years, and
which contains many most interesting references to
the object of their mutual regard.   The first of these
letters remaining refers to a house which Byron had
taken at Hastings, where Hodgson was also staying,

and where the friends had passed many happy hours in one another's society.

My brother desires me to send you the enclosed, and thinks the house was taken from the 13th of July for a month, and therefore that Mr. Barry must have made a mistake in saying the time will have expired *next* Wednesday. You probably can explain this. Pray excuse my being so troublesome.

Yours sincerely,

AUGUSTA LEIGH.

The next letter is dated Newstead Abbey, Sept. 14, 1814.

B. being very lazy, I have requested and obtained permission to write to you, and can only plead in excuse for proposing myself as his substitute, that I have something to say about pupils, and a letter to enclose on the same interesting subject. I have mentioned your wish to several of my friends.[1] I shall hope very soon to hear that you are as happy as I wish *you* and *yours* to be. B. desires to be most kindly remembered. Newstead is *quite his own* again, and Mr. Claughton has forfeited £25,000. Of future plans I really can say nothing,

---

[1] This refers to his intended marriage.

they are in such a glorious state of uncertainty.   I
hope he will write to you of them himself; in the
meantime

Believe me yours most sincerely,

AUGUSTA LEIGH.

From Hastings Hodgson writes in high spirits to
Harry Drury, and again from Cambridge, where he
had gone into residence for the last time.

King's: Sunday.

My dear old Friend,—Is it impossible for you to
come here before the term ends? We could then
pass *our* last days at King's together, and shed a
tear on Haslingfield's green baulks, if baulks be
there still green? Think of this, Master Brooks.
I have a letter from Merivale this morning, can-
vassing for a history of John Sobieski, and accusing
me of excessive 'melancholy, gravity, and refinement!' I was greatly amused with the charges,
having just cut myself shaving from a sudden laugh
when the letter came.   Lonsdale was with me
yesterday and amused me very much by his account of '*the springs rising*' when you were fishing
at Walkerne.   Adieu.

Ever yours,

F. H.

Merivale's charge of 'melancholy,' &c., was endorsed by Byron in a letter to Drury of about the
same date ; but it was only true at times. After
alluding to the near approach of his own marriage,
Byron writes :—

I hope Hodgson is in a fair way on the same voyage.
I saw him and his idol at Hastings. I wish he
would be married at the same time. I should like
to make a party, like people electrified in a row,
by (or rather through) the same chain, holding one
another's hands, and all feeling the shock at once.
I have not yet apprised him of this. He makes
such a serious matter of all these things, and is so
'melancholy and gentlemanlike' that it is quite
overcoming to us choice spirits.

In October of this year Byron met Hodgson in
town, where he stayed only a few days, 'hurried,' as
he says, ' with a thousand things,' and begging to be
excused for ' his haste and laconism ; ' and again at
Cambridge, whence Hodgson wrote to his future wife
an account of their meeting. A fragment of this
letter remains, and is of great interest as containing
contemporary comment upon an event of such vital
importance to those most immediately concerned in
it, and of such world-wide celebrity as the marriage

of Lord and Lady Byron. This fragment also proves the high opinion entertained by Hodgson of his friend's bride, an opinion which remained unaltered until her resolute determination to resist all attempts at reconciliation rendered sympathy with her impossible for anyone who retained his friendship for her husband.

It is most natural that Byron should be absorbed by the thought even, much more by the society, of one of the most divine beings upon earth. He was on his way to Seaham, Sir Ralph Milbanke's seat. His sister, in her last sweet letter, says, ' I have not heard from him for some time, and am uneasy about it ; but it is very selfish to be so, for I know he is happy, and what more can I wish.' Well, on Friday evening, after I had put my letter to you in the post, and one to Harry Drury, and one to my cousin, I was tired with writing, and thought I would go to the coffee-room and read the papers. With nothing then, for the moment, but *Colonel Quintin* and Hanoverianism in my head, I was passing by the Sun Inn, literally passing by it, and at a quick pace, when a carriage and four drove up to the door. A sudden thought struck me ; I cried out ' Byron !' and was answered by a hearty

'Hodgson!' He was about to send to me at King's. He would not have found me there, as I should have been detained for an hour at least with *Colonel Quintin.* Consequently, he would have gone on to his sister's, and I should not have seen him. As it was, we supped together and sate till a late hour over our claret, talking of many and delightful things. He told me *all that could be tola* of his visit to Seaham, and, in a word, for I can say no more if I talk for ever on the subject, he is likely to be *as happy as I am.* Oh! how I glowed with indignation at the base reporters of his *For-tune-hunting.* I will tell you the particulars when we meet. Meanwhile, *entre nous*, he is sacrificing a great deal too much. Not to Miss M.—that is impossible—because nothing is too much for her, and (as is usual in these cases) she would require nothing. But her parents (although B. speaks of them with the most *beautiful* respect) certainly to me appear to be most royally selfish persons. Her fortune is *not* large at present, but he settles £60,000 upon her. This he cannot do *without sell-ing Newstead again* ; and with a look and manner that I cannot easily forget he said : 'You know we must think of these things as little as possible.' 'But,' I replied, 'I am certain, if she saw Newstead she would not let you part with it.' 'Bless her! she has nothing to do with it. Nor would I excite a feeling in her mind that may be prejudicial to her interests.' Now where, where are the hearts of those who can under-value, who can depreciate this man? Besides this, Miss M.'s principal expectations are from Lord Wentworth, her uncle, an old and very infirm man, whom I have often met at Rugby. Perfectly disposed to pay him every respect, B. would not go out of his road to visit him. To meet him he would have been very glad, but he went straight to Miss M. He is returning to town for the purpose of settling all legal affairs, and returns to the North in a fortnight, straight to be married. He fully explained to Miss M. his feeling about Lord W. She was satisfied, and that is enough. As to *herself*, I have much indeed to tell you. The whole story is an interesting one.

B. knows that the lawyers will not be ready for him for this day or two, and therefore, although he was going immediately to London, he means to stay in the neighbourhood till Wednesday to vote for his friend Clark,[1] of Trinity, at the election for the Anatomical Professor. He promised . . . .

[1] The Traveller.

P.S.—I open my letter to say that when Lord Byron went to give his vote just now in the Senate House, the young men burst out into the most rapturous applause.

Mine of yesterday mentioned in the postscript the flattering manner in which Lord Byron was received in the Senate House. I should add that as I was going to vote I met him coming away, and presently saw that something had happened, by his extreme paleness and agitation. Dr. Clark, who was with him, told me the cause, and I returned with B. to my room. There I begged him to sit down and write a letter and communicate this event, which he did not feel up to, but wished *I* would. So down I sate and commenced my acquaintance with Miss Milbanke by writing her an account of this most pleasing event, which, although nothing at Oxford, is here very unusual indeed ; and, as I told you, had occasioned the dismissal of the young men from the Senate House only a few days ago. I also wrote to his sister, and thus I have two more female friends, or one at least, to introduce.

We dined with Dr. Clark and saw a very sweet woman in his wife ; himself the most natural, pleasing, and kind of men. But more upon this subject when we meet. This morning Lord B. and Mr.

Hobhouse departed. B. is to send me word about
—— as a pupil.

A few other remarks occurring in letters of this
date are illustrative of the writer's sentiments on the
different subjects to which they refer.

The first speaks of a change in a friend :—

You can have no conception *now*, what a very sweet
and engaging manner my friend once had. Illness
and affliction will destroy everything, will even turn
the gentle into the *tart and severe* : the most
horrible of all changes in my mind. But I have a
female friend whom I long indeed to introduce to
you. A Herefordshire lady, still called Miss *Hill*,
although now waning into the denomination of
Mrs. Of her more hereafter. This earth does not
hold a better being.

The sweetest line I ever met with (as we are on
the subject—i.e., of epitaphs) is that in Hendon
Churchyard—

> Now my good angel, once my virtuous wife.

The next three letters, written in the year before
Lord Byron's ill-fated marriage, which at first promised such happy results, are full of melancholy
interest.

Sunday, November 13.

Dear Mr. Hodgson,—Thank you a thousand times for your kind congratulations on the approaching marriage, which I hope will secure my dearest B.'s happiness. I had a letter from him on Friday last, in which he says it cannot take place this month or three weeks, and that consequently he shall visit London again in his unmarried state, and bids me expect to hear again from him soon or, perhaps, see him. You probably are aware that he passed through Cambridge[1] a fortnight ago to-day, and I was much surprised to hear slept that night at Wandsford, as when he left me his intention was to do so at Cambridge, and for the purpose of seeing you. Believe me, that it would gratify me sincerely to be of use to you in your present dilemma,[2] for I can enter into the feelings of you and yours most entirely. Byron arrived here late on Saturday night, and set out again soon after he had left his room on Sunday, so that you may imagine I had but a short time to hear and say a thousand things. In answer to an enquiry of mine about you, he

---

[1] This was *before* the visit mentioned above.

[2] This refers to the difficulty experienced by Hodgson in finding a suitable curacy, after giving up his fellowship at King's. He was just at this time contemplating a chaplaincy.

answered that your marriage was still delayed, but nothing more. Mr. Hanson has been at Seaham, and I rather think must now be again in town. Would it be of any use to you if *I* was to write to him on the subject of the chaplaincy? The post between this and Seaham is so dreadfully tedious, and, moreover, you know that B. does not always reply to written enquiries. In spite of this I will write, and also to Mr. H. if you think it better than your writing yourself. I only wish I could hit upon any way of being useful to you. If anything strikes you, pray let me know it immediately, and

Believe me very truly yours,

AUGUSTA LEIGH.

B.'s address is Seaham, Stockton-upon-Tees, Durham.

Six Mile Bottom : November 24.

Dear Mr. Hodgson,—Many thanks for your welcome intelligence, which it was kind of you to communicate. Poor B.! he must, I think, have been disturbed. I think I see him—and it gives me quite a nervous sensation. I would not have you think that I have forgot *your* concerns, but not one syllable of answer have I got from Mr. H. As far as regards myself this does not signify, but I am rather angry with him for keeping you in suspense. I suppose B. is gone, so I dare not enclose to him. I trust, indeed, there is everything to hope for his happiness, and, as you say, Newstead is the only drop of bitter in the cup. I try to banish it from my *thoughts*, but I cannot from my *dreams*, where it haunts me eternally. Alas! I see no remedy, but I never like to despair, and you would smile at my irrational hopes. Col. Leigh appears ·to think it not impossible we may have the pleasure of seeing you here by-and-bye. I need not say what pleasure it would give me. In the mean time

Believe me,

Truly yours,

A. L.

Seaham : November 25, 1814.

Dear Sir,—It will be easier for you to imagine than for me to express the pleasure which your very kind letter has given me. Not only on account of its gratifying intelligence, but also as introductory to an acquaintance which I have been taught to value, and have sincerely desired. Allow me to consider Lord Byron's friend as not 'a stranger,' and accept, with my sincerest thanks, my best wishes for your own happiness.

I am, dear Sir,

Your faithful servant,

A. I. MILBANKE.

END OF THE FIRST VOLUME.

LONDON : PRINTED BY
SPOTTISWOODE AND CO., NEW-STREET SQUARE
AND PARLIAMENT STREET

9 783744 691765